FATHER
TURIDDU

A NOVEL

Daniel Conway

FATHER
TURIDDU

A NOVEL

Riverwood Press
Louisville, KY

Front cover illustration:

The flag of Sicily was first adopted in A.D. 1282, after the successful Sicilian Vespers revolt. It is characterized by the presence of the triskelion (*trinacria*) in its middle, the (winged) head of Medusa and three wheat ears. The three bent legs are said to represent the three points of the triangular shape of the island of Sicily itself. The present design became the official public flag of the Autonomous Region of Sicily on January 4, 2000.

Back cover illustration:

The Sicilian Cart (*carretto siciliano*)
An ornate, colorful style of horse or donkey-drawn cart native to the island of Sicily.

Published by: Riverwood Press Louisville, KY

ISBN 978-0615769554

Cover and interior design by Jane Lee
Sketches by Mark Castillo, Copy editing by William R. Bruns

Printed and bound in the United States of America

DEDICATION

This book is dedicated to the Reverend Monsignor
Salvatore E. Polizzi, pastor of St. Roch Catholic Church
in St. Louis, Mo., in gratitude for his friendship, gener-
osity and extraordinary dedication to his family, friends,
community and Church.

AUTHOR'S NOTE

This is a work of fiction. While it's true that certain characters have been inspired by real people, all of the situations, events and conversations contained in this story are the work of my imagination. Names have been changed (ever so slightly) to protect the innocent.

DAY ONE.

Monsignor Salvatore E. Turiddu
(Father T)

DAY ONE.
MORNING.

The threat was real. And deadly.

At exactly 9 a.m., an ominous message appeared on the computer screen of every city worker (including police and firefighters), every union leader, every newspaper, and radio and TV station in the city. A printed copy was delivered by courier to the Office of the Mayor. It said:

DEATH TO THE ABORTIONISTS. IN 5 DAYS— AT THE CONCLUSION OF THE FIFTH DAY— AT THE STROKE OF MIDNIGHT—EVERY EVERY ABORTION PROVIDER IN THE CITY WILL BE OUT OF BUSINESS PERMANENTLY. EVERYONE WHO WORKS IN ONE OF THESE DEATH FACTORIES WILL LEARN BY EXPERIENCE THE FATE OF AN ABORTED UNBORN CHILD. YOU CAN SHUT DOWN THE CLINICS (THE SOONER THE BETTER) BUT YOU CAN'T STOP US FROM DESTROY- ING THEM. YOU CAN RUN BUT YOU CAN'T HIDE. WE KNOW WHERE YOU LIVE.

All attempts to discover the source of the message or the identity of the sender(s) had failed. In fact, the skill used to deliver this terrorist threat was incredible. Theoretically, it couldn't be done. City workers were all connected by a central database, but not the various unions representing both government and business employees. And certainly not the media outlets scattered throughout the region. Whoever sent this message was highly skilled with amazing technical resources. Whoever sent this message was serious. Perhaps deadly so.

The mayor called the commissioner of police immediately. The commissioner called the U.S. attorney and the FBI. Threats against abortion clinics are considered hate crimes—federal offenses. All available local, state and federal resources were set in motion. If successful, the threat would destroy four abortion clinics and murder nearly 500 employees, an average of 125 per clinic if all personnel were included. That would amount to a terrorist attack of major proportions. It would also be an embarrassment to the city. And the nation.

An emergency meeting was held in the mayor's office at city hall. The mood was somber. All efforts to identify the source of the message had failed. Television's crime scene dramas may dazzle audiences the world over with scientific instruments that can produce clues with microscopic accuracy, but in real life things aren't, so simple. In spite of their best efforts, and the FBI's extensive database in Washington, D.C., city investigators and the FBI had to admit they were literally clueless about the source and the substance of the threat they faced. Even the Department of Homeland Security, the agency created to coordinate efforts to prevent terrorist attacks from both foreign and domestic sources, was unable to provide any helpful information.

The U.S. attorney spoke first in a high-pitched voice that confirmed the police commissioner's impression of him as a nervous little man with no real law enforcement experience and no appreciation of the challenges faced by city police officers every day. In fact, the U.S. attorney had more than a dozen years on the job as an assistant prosecutor, but it was in a smaller city (in another state) with a modest crime rate and few, if any, substantial terrorist threats.

"It has to be a group of religious fanatics—one of those violent anti-abortion groups," the U.S, attorney nearly screamed. "What kind of intel do we have on right-wing religious organizations in the region?"

The police commissioner could barely contain himself. A veteran of more than 30 years with the city's police department, he'd seen and heard everything. "Every pro-life organization in the city and county is being checked out carefully. If any of their members are responsible for this, we'll know about it. We have inside connections in all these groups. We know what they're planning before they do!"

The FBI's chief field agent agreed. "We monitor the national groups as well. This is someone new—either a very talented individual who's figured out how to hack into several unconnected systems or a renegade group we're not aware of that has incredible resources."

The mayor asked the question that was on everyone's mind. "How serious is this threat?" He knew that his political career was on the line no matter how many federal agencies got involved. "And what are we going to do about it? We have a press conference scheduled for noon today, and the ravenous media wolves will want some assurance we're on top of this."

All necessary precautions are being taken," the police commissioner said. "We've closed all the clinics and locked them up tight. No one gets inside without our knowledge."

"What about the employees?" the U.S. attorney asked. The message says they'll be tracked down and killed no matter where they go. Is that really possible? What about witness protection?"

"Not realistic," the FBI's chief field agent said. "By the time we processed them all, the five-day deadline would be long past. We can't hide 500 people on such short notice. "

The mayor sighed deeply. He had been a smoker for 25 years but gave up the habit three years earlier when he ran for office. Now he really wanted a cigarette. "We have five days to find out who we're dealing with and prevent a catastrophe. Let's not waste any more time talking. Let's get busy and find these terrorists—whoever they are!"

The meeting was over. As the police commissioner stood up, he said to the mayor, "I'm going to call Father T."

"Good idea," said the mayor. "He has connections in this city that go back before any of us were born. When

Father T wants something, he gets it."

"Who's Father T?" the U.S. attorney asked the FBI's chief field agent as they left the room together.

"That's Father Turiddu, a Catholic priest. He's called *il salvatore della città*, the savior of the city."

"Savior of the city? Why?" The U.S. attorney's voice rose another octave.

"Many reasons," the police commissioner said. "Ask anyone from the Italian neighborhood or any police officer or city employee. They'll tell you that in this town no one commands greater respect than Father T."

The U.S attorney decided not to ask any more questions. He had to admit that the transition to a new position—a promotion that he'd waited many years to get—was often frustrating. The city was a place of mystery, some might say madness, and he often felt like he was on the outside looking in. He desperately wanted to identify and disarm this new terrorist group. That would show everyone why he was the U.S attorney, a man to be reckoned with, and respected, more than any Catholic priest.

DAY ONE.
AFTERNOON.

Father T was in the kitchen preparing the ingredients for his signature dish, Pasta Turiddu, when the police commissioner called.

"I'm having friends over to the rectory for supper," he explained. "We'll have a drink in the front room and chit-chat for a while. Then we'll have my pasta, Veal Spiedini the way my mother used to make it and home-made cannoli for dessert. I don't bake the cannoli shells anymore. Who has the time! But I make the crème filling just the way my sister taught me, and I have a friend bring shells fresh from the Italian bakery."

"Father, I don't mean to interrupt, but we have a serious problem," the police commissioner said. "A terrorist group that we can't identify is threatening to destroy all the abortion clinics in the city. Hundreds of employees' lives are at risk if we don't stop them in the next five days."

"I know about the messages on the computers at city hall," the priest said. "My secretary's brother works for the department of parks and recreation. He called me right away. So did several union leaders and my friends in the media. The editor of that rag we call a newspaper can't stand me. (He refuses to print anything I send him.) But several of his reporters are my parishioners. They keep me in the loop."

"We need your help, Father." People who knew him well rarely called Father Turiddu by his formal title, *Monsignor*, although he had been a monsignor—officially a member of the papal household—for many years. He preferred it that way. The archdiocese waited too long to recommend him to the Holy See. By the time he was made a monsignor, his mother had already died. "What's the point," he used to say. "It was important to her, not to me." As a result, he always called himself "Father."

"We can't stop them unless we know who they are, Father. All our sources have dried up on this one. They either don't know or they're not talking."

"I'll see what I can find out," Father T told the commissioner, "but it won't be easy. Whoever's doing this is smart, highly organized and well funded. I'll say a special prayer to the Sacred Heart. He's my main man in tough situations. He's gotten me out of more jackpots than I can count!"

"I have to hang up now, Commissioner," the priest said. "It's time for me to go to the nursing home to see my sister. Then I have to stop by the chancery and talk to the archbishop about a young priest who needs a new assignment. They placed him in a small parish in the country. I had to look it up on the map! He won't learn anything there. Besides, he speaks fluent

Italian from his years of study in Rome. We need him in the Italian parish!"

"Thank you, Father," the police commissioner said. He grew up in the Italian parish when Father T was one of three priests assigned there. He knew the priest was right about the need. He also suspected Father T would find a way to get the young priest assigned there. Most of all, he had faith in Father T's connections and his ability to get information when no one else could.

"We're counting on you, Father. Ciao!"

Before he left for the nursing home, Father T called Louis Lombardi, an old friend from his days as an urban planner.

"Lou, this is Father. What's the word on the street about the abortion clinics? Any idea who's behind this?"

"Not a clue. Either no one knows or no one is willing to talk. That worries me. Either these guys are so smart they've managed to stay hidden from everyone or they're so bad that no one will risk crossing them."

"What if they're both," Father T said. "What if they're smart as the devil and meaner than hell!"

"Then we're in big trouble. I'll keep digging, Father. We're bound to find something."

"Do that, Lou. It's important that we be consistent in our defense of life. I don't like what those clinics do to desperate women and their unborn babies, but violence is never the answer. All life is sacred, and no one has the right to play God. End of story!"

"You know I'll do what I can, Father."

"You're a good friend, Lou. Thank you. Will we see you in church this Sunday? We miss you."

Lou mumbled something about a meeting he was late for and hung up. Father T didn't really expect to see him that weekend, but the seed was planted.

At the nursing home, Father T visited Jenny, one of his three surviving sisters. The Turiddu family originally included his parents and their four sons and seven daughters. Salvatore Emmanuel, now Father T or Uncle Sal to his many nieces, nephews, grandnieces and grandnephews, was the youngest. But with only 4 of the original family members still alive, Father T at 81 had now become the head of the family.

"Thank God I have my health," Father T always said. "For nearly 80 years, until my brother Dominic died last year, my family took care of me. Now it's payback time."

Father T had a passion for his family—and also for his Church, his neighborhood and his city. But family was first. One day many years earlier, when he visited his oldest sister, Philomena, in the hospital, she could tell he was in a bad mood and feeling sorry for himself.

"Did you go to Catholic school?" his sister asked unexpectedly.

"You know I did, Phil," the priest answered.

"Who paid for it?"

"Ma did."

"And did you go to college and to the seminary and to graduate school?" his sister asked.

"You know I did. Why are you asking me these questions?"

"Who paid for your education?"

"You know that Ma paid for my education," the priest said.

"You've been blessed, Salvatore. Now it's payback time."

Father T vowed he would never forget those words as long as he lived: *Now it's payback time!*

Family, Church, neighborhood, city. These were the circles Father T traveled in, the worlds he inhabited. All had been good to him. As long as he lived, he would work to pay off the debts he felt he owed them.

Many people would have said that the debts were long since paid and that what Father T gave back far exceeded what he was given in the first place. There was no question that he had earned the respect of others. His influence was powerful and his ability to get things done was legendary. He was once offered an important position in the Carter administration because of his skill in urban planning, but Father T declined. "I'm a parish priest," he said. "I have no business doing anything but this."

Father T believed that nothing was more important than being a good pastor. He said he learned this early in his priesthood from the good Fathers who were his mentors. He was a parish priest—first and foremost. His calling was to be Christ for others in whatever situation he found himself.

Being Christ for others wasn't always what people expected. One day, when he was organizing a protest against the way the new interstate highway was going to divide the Italian neighborhood, a woman said to him, "Father, I thought Jesus said we should turn the other cheek when someone offends us."

"I'm not Jesus," Father T responded. "And there's no way I'm going to let a bunch of government bureaucrats destroy this neighborhood. We're going to fight back. And we're going to win!"

The issue was a bridge over the new highway that was not part of the original plans. Father T insisted that an overpass was needed to allow firefighters and other emergency personnel access to the neighborhood when trains had all the other streets blocked.

"Without that overpass, people will die," Father T, said. "So unless they build it, we're going to make sure the highway never opens."

To the astonishment of the government bureaucrats, the construction company that was awarded the contract agreed. The company stopped working on that section of the highway and waited for a decision about the overpass. What the government didn't know was that the people in the neighborhood—encouraged by Father T—had made a special point of befriending the workers, bringing them food and refreshments and making them feel completely at home in their community. They all knew that Father T was serious, and they did whatever he asked. In the end, the neighborhood was saved.

Il salvatore della città, they called him then. But could he do it again now?

Father T headed to the chancery to see the archbishop. On the way, he called his niece Anna using the Bluetooth feature that connected his cell phone to his car's audio system. Pedestrians crossing in front of him at the red light were understandably concerned. What they *saw* was a distinguished looking priest in a Roman collar gesturing broadly in the Italian style to his steering wheel. What they *heard,* even with the windows closed, were instructions shouted at the top of his voice in response to the Bluetooth system's voice prompts.

"Please say a command," a woman's voice said matter-of-factly.

"DIAL!" the priest responded.

"Please say the name of the person you are calling," the voice continued.

"ANNA!" the pedestrians heard him shout.

"Please repeat the name of the person you are calling," said the woman's voice which was either very hard of hearing or suffering from the effects of an unfortunate blip in the cell phone's transmission.

"ANNA!" the priest shouted once again. "I SAID ANNA!"

Just then, the light turned green and Father T continued down the road—accelerating to more than 20 miles above the speed limit before catching himself and applying the breaks until he had slowed down to exactly 5 miles above the legal limit. He wasn't worried about getting a speeding ticket—no police officer in the city would have dared to cite Father T—but he didn't need the aggravation of being pulled over only to be sent on his way as soon as he was recognized.

Still shouting, he left a message on his niece's voice mail. "ANNA, THIS IS UNCLE SAL. CALL ME, PLEASE. IT'S IMPORTANT."

Anna Dominica had connections her uncle didn't. She was a businesswoman trained in accounting and financial planning. She counseled many nonprofit organizations on their investments, and she was an active member of the archdiocese's pro-life committee. Father T wanted to make sure that Anna used her connections to help find out who was behind this new terrorist group.

The priest arrived at the chancery just in time for his 4 o'clock appointment with the archbishop. There was not enough time for him to make his usual rounds. Whenever he was in the building, Father T made a point of paying his respects to the most important people on the church's payroll—the secretaries who staffed the various offices and agencies of the archdiocese. From many years' experience, Father T knew that paying a little attention to the gatekeepers (greeting them with a smile and asking about their families) always paid big dividends. He not only got the local gossip before anyone else; when he needed a favor or an appointment, he was always at the head of the line.

"Good afternoon, Archbishop. Thank you for seeing me on short notice."

"Good afternoon, Monsignor. How are your sisters today?" The archbishop was always personable and down to earth, a "pastoral" bishop in spite of his degree in canon law and many years as an administrator. After more than 25 years as a bishop, he was always attentive to the personal lives of his priests.

"I thank God for your good health, Monsignor, and your service to your parish and the archdiocese well beyond the age when most priests have retired."

"God has been good to me, Archbishop, and I must do what I can to be a good steward and return his gifts with increase."

"Now, Monsignor, how can I help you?"

"I'll come right to the point, Archbishop. The Italian parish needs an associate who speaks the language. My young cousin is a beloved pastor, but he can only do so much." Father T's 60-year-old cousin, Msgr. Vincent Cugino, had served as pastor of the Italian parish for more than a decade. A second generation Italian American, he didn't speak Italian and really did need help—especially with the hundreds of weddings and funerals that were celebrated for those who grew up in the Italian neighborhood but had moved away only to come back again at special moments in their lives (baptisms, marriages and funerals).

"Did you have someone in mind, Monsignor?"

"The young man who just returned from Rome would be perfect for the Italian parish. He speaks the language almost as well as I do."

"But you know that Father already has an assignment," said the Archbishop wearing the poker face he adopted when discussing personnel matters.

"Yes, but forgive me for being blunt, Archbishop. It's a waste of talent sending this young man to a country parish. He should be in the city where his pastoral skills will be formed and tested. You know that it takes a special talent to minister to the Italian parish. I was there for 25 years, Archbishop. I know what it takes out of you—and what it gives back. Vince—excuse me, Archbishop, I mean Monsignor Cugino—is exhausted. He really needs the help."

"Let me look into it, Monsignor, and we'll see what we can do."

"Thank you, Archbishop. That's all I ask."

"Now, tell me about this domestic terrorist threat everyone's talking about. The mayor tells me they've asked you for help."

"I'm asking around, Archbishop. I think funding may be the key. I hope my niece Anna can help me find out where the money is coming from."

"Do whatever you can, Monsignor. I told the mayor that the archdiocese will help the city in every way possible. We oppose all threats against life wherever they come from and no matter who the target is. Just today the Holy Father issued a statement that reinforces our Church's position on life. His subject was stem-cell research, but the points he made are equally valid. 'Saving one life cannot justify destroying another,' the pope said. That is certainly true in this case!"

"You can count on me, Archbishop."

"I know it, Monsignor. Please give my best to your sisters. They are in my prayers."

"Thank you, Archbishop. Please come for supper soon. I'll prepare the veal just the way you like it and, of course, we'll have my Pasta Turiddu!"

Sounds delicious, Monsignor. *La pace di Cristo con voi.*"

"*E con il tuo spirito, Eccellenza!*"

DAY ONE.
EVENING.

Father T returned to the rectory in time to prepare supper. Cooking relaxed him. Taught by his oldest sister, Philomena, he took delight in the whole process—from selecting and preparing the ingredients to the art of cooking and the joy of sharing his favorite meals with family and friends.

His guests that evening were two priests—his cousin Msgr. Cugino, pastor of the Italian parish, and Msgr. John Dutzow, a friend and former associate, who now served as pastor of a struggling city parish. The third guest was a layman who worked for the archdiocese as a planning consultant. The layman was a long-time friend of Father T. He didn't say much at these gatherings, but he listened intently and took mental notes as the priests discussed archdiocesan and city politics.

The threat against the four abortion clinics was the main topic of conversation during drinks in the front room. Each priest made his own drink from Father T's ample supply of liquor and mixes. The layman drank Crodino, a nonalcoholic fruit drink that Father T brought home from Italy in his suitcase (a ten-pack of small bottles). Crodino is not generally available in the United States, but Father T had searched for it on the Internet and found it listed for sale at an Italian import store in Pittsburgh called Pennsylvania Macaroni. He planned to call the store in Pittsburgh when he had the time to see if the aperitif could be shipped to him.

Msgr. Cugino argued with his older cousin about the so-called terrorist group. "It's one person—a mentally disturbed individual who's figured out how to hack into several computer systems simultaneously. I'm not saying he's harmless—far from it—but I don't believe there's a whole group of people behind this."

Msgr. Dutzow was the "agnostic" in the room. Trained as a scientist—a former biology teacher—he was inclined to wait for hard evidence before reaching any conclusion. "The fact is we have practically nothing to work with here. An untraceable message on a bunch of computer screens doesn't tell us anything. I agree that law enforcement has to take this threat seriously—and consider every possibility—but it's a mistake to jump to any conclusions."

Father T excused himself to check on supper. While he was in the kitchen his cell phone rang. It was Anna returning his call.

"I can't talk now, Anna. I'm about to serve my pasta. Can I call you later tonight?"

"Yes, Uncle Sal, but don't forget. I have some information for you that you'll want to hear."

"I won't forget," Father T said. "I'll call you as soon as we finish supper and have cleaned up the kitchen. I promise it won't be late."

When the priest returned to his guests, they had moved on to a different subject. The archdiocese was planning an increase in the assessment, or tax, paid by every parish. The increase was intended to help more families afford to send their children to Catholic schools. The pastors agreed it was a worthy goal, but they tended to be skeptical about increasing the assessment—especially during a recession!

"Throwing money at a problem never solves anything," said Msgr. Dutzow whose school had closed just before he became pastor following an unsuccessful attempt to merge with another parish school nearby. "The real problem is that parents today don't value Catholic education the way they used to. They don't bring their kids to Mass on Sunday, and they don't participate in parish activities or contribute to the Sunday collection. How will an increase in the assessment help that? It's just robbing Peter to pay Paul.

"I don't disagree with you," said Msgr. Cugino. "We have an excellent school, but it's a struggle to keep our parents involved. They say they want their children raised Catholic, but they want us to do it all for them. Unfortunately, it doesn't work that way."

"We have the best school in the city," said Father T. "If you want to send your children to our school, you have to participate. And if you're Catholic, you have to bring them with you to Mass. I know everyone who's in church on weekends—and everyone who isn't. If you can't afford our tuition, we'll help you out. No child is refused because his parents can't pay—but only if they are active members of the parish community. End of story!"

Dinner was served family style in the rectory dining room surrounded by elegant oil paintings of peasants in native dress in the Sicilian countryside. All of the furnishings in the dining room and the front room belonged to Father T personally. They were either gifts from family members or friends or beautiful pieces that the priest and ladies of the parish bought at bargain prices at estate sales all over the city. "You should see what was here when I first moved in 30 years ago," he would say. "It's all stored in the attic. If the man who succeeds me here doesn't appreciate nice things, I'll take all my furnishings with me. I'll bring all that junk down from the attic, and the new man will inherit this place exactly as I found it 30 years ago!"

First the Pasta Turiddu. Then Veal Spiedini with onion and bay leaves fresh from Father T's garden. And then salad (after the meal to help with digestion and ready the palate for dessert). Once the table was cleared, with Msgr. Cugino rinsing the dishes and loading the dishwasher and Msgr. Dutzow and the layman clearing the table and helping Father T put things away, the cannoli was served. The sweet crème filling could only be described as heavenly, a taste to die for, especially at the end of a wonderful meal.

The guests didn't stay long. The priests all had

early morning Masses and the layman said he had a breakfast meeting. Once he was sure that everything had been put away properly and the alarm was set for the night, Father T went upstairs to his sitting room. This was his personal space where he was surrounded by photographs and books and mementos of the past 81 years. A friend from the Italian parish had installed a gas fireplace the week Father T moved in to this once dying but now thriving parish 30 years ago. Here he could relax and read and pray.

The clock in Father's sitting room said it was 9 p.m.—plenty of time to call Anna. He reached her at home, where she was still working on a client's tax return.

"What do you have for me, Anna?"

"Some interesting news, Uncle Sal. There's a new nonprofit group that's filed for tax-exempt status called *Defensores Libertatis* (Defenders of Freedom). They're an offshoot of a pro-life group that's been around a long time called *Defensores Vitae* (Defenders of Life).

"I know that group," the priest said. "They've always been nonviolent. They're not affiliated with any church in spite of the Latin name."

"Yes, but apparently some of their newer members became impatient and began advocating violence. They were expelled from the original organization and ended up forming a splinter group that is definitely more aggressive in its rhetoric. There's nothing I know of to suggest they're behind yesterday's computer message, but they're worth watching just the same.

"Thanks, Anna. I'll call the commissioner first thing tomorrow and let him know. When are you going to visit Aunt Anne?"

"I'm taking her to lunch tomorrow, Uncle Sal, like I do every week."

"She'll be glad to see you, Anna."

"I know, Uncle Sal. I know."

When she was younger, Father T's sister Anne had been very prominent in the city's social circles. She was a contributing member of hundreds of charitable organizations, and she attended every charity event— the fancier the better. The other members of Father T's family didn't know what to make of her. Theirs was a much simpler way of life. "But it's her money," Father T always said. "Let her spend it the way she wants to."

Now in her 90s and infirm, Anne didn't get out much. Father T made sure she had the very best home health care available, and he constantly reminded his nieces and nephews to visit their Aunt Anne. His niece Anna didn't need reminding. As her namesake, Anna was devoted to her Aunt Anne. But Father T reminded her anyway. He couldn't help himself. As head of the family now, it was his job to make sure everyone did his or her part for the good of all!

DAY TWO.

Monsignor Vincent Cugino
*(Father T's cousin, pastor of
the Italian parish)*

DAY TWO.
MORNING.

As soon as he said the morning Mass, Father Turiddu called the police commissioner. Daily Mass was celebrated in a small chapel in the school building (a former classroom). Father T refused to heat or air condition the whole church when only a handful of people came to daily Mass.

"Commissioner, this is Father. My niece Anna says there's a new anti-abortion group called Defenders of Freedom—an offshoot of Defenders of Life. She thinks you should look into them."

"Thanks, Father. As far as I know, this group is not on our radar screen. Anything to suggest they're behind this threat?"

"Only that they appear to be more radical than Defenders of Life. Anna says they are impatient with the older group's lack of progress. They want to end abortion now. Of course, I agree with them, but the end doesn't justify the means!"

"We'll check them out, Father. Thanks for the tip."

"You're welcome, Commissioner. Let me know what you find. I have a funeral at the Italian parish at 11 followed by lunch with a young priest who's asked for my help. I'll be back here at the rectory around 2 o'clock."

Father T drank his coffee and read the newspaper from cover to cover. The local news interested him most (followed by the obituaries), especially coverage of the new terrorist threat. As usual, the newspaper got the moral issues wrong. Determined to portray everything as either black or white (conservative or liberal), the newspaper's editorial page attacked *all* pro-life organizations, accusing them of "creating a climate of hate" that encouraged "extreme right-wing radicals." Organizations like Planned Parenthood were praised for their "courageous service to the community." That made the priest's Sicilian blood boil!

Father T's secretary was used to hearing him argue out loud while reading the newspaper in the kitchen. If he shouted loudly enough, or if his one-way conversation lasted long enough, she knew there was a good chance he would come into the office, sit down at the computer and compose a letter to the editor. The priest knew they wouldn't print anything he sent them, but he felt better once the letter was composed, printed, signed and mailed.

In his younger days, when he was an associate at the Italian parish, Father T succeeded in getting a promise in writing from the newspaper's publisher that the word *mafia* would never appear in stories written by local reporters. (The publisher said he had no control over stories supplied by the wire services.) Father T had gathered signatures from prominent Italian-Americans (including one of the newspaper's largest advertisers) in support of a statement that maintained the word *mafia* was an ethnic slur that impugned the integrity of an entire community.

"We're not interested in protecting the criminal activities of a few individuals," Father T told the publisher. "Go ahead and print their names if you want to. But that word—I refuse to say it—implicates all of us, including my mother and my family, and we're not going to stand for it!"

As the years went by, new reporters or careless editors occasionally slipped and the forbidden word would appear in a local story. When that happened, management heard about it right away—either from Msgr. Cugino, the pastor of St. Ambrose, the Italian parish, or one of the leaders of the Italian-American community. The offensive word was immediately removed from the newspaper's online edition, and the reporter and editor each received a sharply worded rebuke from the Office of the Publisher.

Today, Father T had no time for letters. He had to stop at the seminary on his way to the funeral. As the executor of a former classmate's rather complicated estate, Father T was responsible for distributing all his friend's personal property, including a collection of rare books that Father T thought should be given to the seminary library in honor of his classmate. He wanted to speak personally to the rector and the head librarian to make sure that his friend's collection would be given the prominence it deserved. The alternative was to give the books to the Jesuits. That was an option Father T did not intend to exercise, but he wanted the seminary's leaders to know it was a possibility.

By the time he arrived at the restaurant for his lunch meeting, Father T was worn out. His meetings at the seminary had lasted longer than he planned, and although the rector and head librarian were most gracious, assuring him that his classmate's rare books would receive a place of honor, he left feeling frustrated. Had he known how much work would be required, he never would have agreed to serve as executor of his classmate's estate—or so he told himself in moments of frustration.

The funeral had gone smoothly. Msgr. Cugino said the Mass and he preached the homily. Father T gave the final commendation and said a few words at the end of Mass. He knew the deceased man from the old neighborhood, and he was able to tell stories that consoled the family and made the large congregation of relatives and friends feel at home. Father T did not go to the cemetery. That would have taken another hour out of his busy day—but he knew the family was in good hands with Msgr. Cugino, "the kid."

The Osteria was one of three restaurants owned and operated by the Norcini family on the city's south side. All the staff knew Father T, and they greeted him warmly with hugs and kisses. The proprietor, Bart Norcini, knew that Father T liked sweet potatoes, so in spite of the fact that they were not on the menu, he kept a special supply of sweet potatoes in the kitchen just for Father T.

The young priest was already seated at the corner table reserved for Father T. As he walked to the table, he was stopped by several people from the Italian neighborhood who remembered him from the old days more than 30 years ago. "Please come back and visit us, Father. We miss you. Things have not been the same since you left us!"

When he finally broke away from his former parishioners, Father T got a good look at his lunch guest, and he was not happy. The young priest was wearing a cassock—the long dark robe that priests of Father T's generation (and several generations after him) had hoped was gone forever. No such luck. The young men wore them all the time now—and in places like this restaurant that Father T thought were totally inappropriate.

"Monsignor Turiddu, thank you for meeting me today," the young priest said.

"You're welcome, Father, but please tell me why you're wearing that outfit."

"My cassock? In the seminary, we wore them all the time. It was strongly encouraged."

"Well you're not in the seminary now. Or in church. Or in the schoolyard. The next time I see you out in public dressed like this, I'm going to call the archbishop."

"I'm very sorry, Monsignor. Had I known how you feel about this, I never would have worn my cassock today. Please accept my sincere apology."

"Never mind that. There's no need to apologize to me, Father. Let's enjoy our lunch. The filet of sole is exceptional here. So is the risotto."

The young priest tried the sole and immediately agreed with his host who turned out to be much more agreeable after he had eaten one of the Norcini family's specialty dishes. Father T drank an Arnold Palmer (half lemonade and half iced tea), but he persuaded his young companion to have a glass of white wine with his fish.

After they finished their meal, and all the dishes were cleared, Father T said, "OK, young man. What did you want to talk to me about?"

"I'm afraid I'm in trouble, Monsignor, and my pastor urged me to talk to you. He said you have helped other priests get out of tough situations." The young priest spoke softly not wanting his conversation to be heard by people seated at nearby tables.

"We're here to help each other, Father. Tell me what the problem is."

"Well, I've been in this parish—the largest one in the archdiocese—for just over a year now since my ordination. When I first arrived, I met a young man from the parish, and we became friends."

"How old was he," Father T asked. "And how old are you?"

"I'm 27, and he told me he was 18, but I later found out that wasn't true. He had just turned 17 at the time we met. That means his 18th birthday was just a couple of weeks ago."

"Please tell me what happened," Father T said.

"At first, everything was fine. We went to a ballgame and saw some movies. We had pizza and cokes, and we talked about sports and about the girls he had dated. (He said he was in-between girlfriends.) But nothing happened that could remotely be considered inappropriate until we'd been friends for about six months."

"Go on, Father. Everything you tell me will be kept in strict confidence—like the seal of Confession."

"Well, one night we went to see a late movie. In the dark theater, with no one seated around us, he put his hand on me and began to massage my leg and my private parts. I was so surprised I just sat there—horrified and very embarrassed! When I finally realized what was happening—it couldn't have lasted more than 30 seconds—I stood up and left the theater. Fortunately, he didn't come with me. (I wouldn't have known what to say to him.) So I went back to the rectory and went to bed, but it took a long time for me to get any sleep that night."

"So what's the problem, now? Have you had any contact with this young man since that night? Obviously something is bothering you."

"I haven't seen him or talked to him since that night. He stopped coming around the parish and, frankly, I was glad that I didn't have to confront him. We had some mutual acquaintances, but they didn't know where he was either. Someone suggested he had gone to the university to get his degree, but no one seemed to know for sure. I never did know his family or where he lived."

"You were friends for six months, but you didn't know where he lived or who his family was?"

"With hindsight I know it seems odd, but at the time I never thought about it. We weren't really close friends, just buddies who did things together."

"I understand," said the older priest. "You're a young man. As we get older we learn to pay more attention to these things. So, what's happened now?"

Two days ago I got a letter from an attorney. The letter says that my friend is in jail—it doesn't say why—and that he wants to see me, in the attorney's words, 'to protect my reputation.' According to the letter, my so-called friend is implying that our relationship was sexual, which it absolutely was not! I immediately talked to my pastor, and showed him the letter. That's when he suggested I talk to you."

"Can I see the letter?" Father T asked.

"Of course, Monsignor. I made a copy for you." The young priest handed him a photocopy.

The letter, which was written on the attorney's stationery was brief but designed to intimidate—especially with its intimation of a sexual relationship between the priest and the young man now residing in the city jail. That tactic didn't work with Father T. He knew the attorney by reputation, but, more importantly, he recognized the name of the client who purportedly wanted to protect the young priest's reputation.

"Don't worry about this, Father. We'll take care of it. Go back to your parish and make no attempt to contact this young man. If his attorney calls you, give him my phone number (the rectory number, not my cell phone) and tell him that from now on he has to deal with me. End of story."

"I'm so grateful, Monsignor. Thank you. My pastor said you would help me."

"Pay close attention to your pastor, Father. He's a good man and you can learn a lot from him—including when and where to wear your cassock."

"I don't think he wears his cassock very often," the young priest said sheepishly.

"Exactly. Now go on with you. I have a lot of work to do this afternoon."

DAY TWO.
AFTERNOON.

The mayor was not in a good mood. The new terrorist threat was all he'd heard about for the past day and a half. Everyone expected answers, and decisive action, but he had nothing to give them. No answers and no decisions. Just the ongoing investigation.

And the investigation was driving him crazy. Collaborating with the U.S. attorney was a real pain. He insisted on coordinating—actually controlling—everything, but as an outsider he didn't know the community. They were wasting lots of time traveling down blind alleys and scrutinizing individuals and groups that no one familiar with the city would have bothered with. The FBI was not nearly so difficult to work with, but the feds had their own strict protocols for everything and communication with the FBI was rarely a two-way street.

Thank God for the police commissioner. Like the mayor, he was born and raised in the city. As Father T would say, he knew the territory. The mayor and the commissioner didn't always agree, but that was to be expected. The mayor was a political animal—always conscious of the possible future implications of what he said or did. The commissioner was a career police officer. He did what he thought was right, or at least what he believed he had to do in the current situation. Let the mayor worry about reelection. The commissioner's priorities were serving and protecting—his city and his department—by whatever means were necessary. The mayor knew he could trust the commissioner. He wasn't so sure about the U.S. attorney or the FBI.

"Mr. Mayor!" His secretary screamed from the outer office. "There's another message from the terrorists!"

The mayor grabbed the mouse in front of his computer, and the screen immediately came alive. Sure enough, there was another message, and this one was more ominous than the first one.

DEATH TO THE ABORTIONISTS!

WE WILL KEEP OUR PROMISES.

IN FOUR DAYS—AT THE STROKE OF MIDNIGHT AT THE END OF THE FIFTH DAY— ABORTION WILL BE HISTORY AND ALL ABORTIONISTS WILL EXPERIENCE THE FATE OF THEIR INNOCENT VICTIMS.

ALL EFFORTS TO STOP US ARE POINTLESS.

WE WILL KEEP OUR PROMISES.

The mayor reached for the telephone, but before he could place a call, his secretary informed him that the police commissioner was on line 1.

"I was just about to call you," the mayor said. "You've

seen the latest message?"

"Yes, sir, I have. We're checking to see who else received it, but it's definitely on every computer screen in our building and yours."

"Why can't we stop this? It makes us look like complete idiots and it compromises the integrity of all our confidential files."

"Our electronic security people are working with the FBI experts, but we still don't know how the intruders are getting into our systems. Until we know the source of the problem, there's not much we can do to prevent these cyber attacks."

"Find out if the media got this latest message," the mayor said in his most irritated tone of voice. "Yesterday's press conference was a disaster—as you well know. The next time I have to face those vultures, I better have some meat to give them or I'm going to turn them over to you."

The mayor immediately regretted his last statement. There was no telling what the commissioner might say to the media. He might just tell them the truth—that we don't have a clue who's behind this or how they're doing it.

"We're pursuing a lead Father T gave us. There's a new anti-abortion group that seems to be more radical than any of the others, but so far we can't connect them to the computer messages."

"Dig deeper, commissioner. We need answers—now!"

"I understand, sir. You'll know the minute we have anything solid."

"It doesn't have to be solid, commissioner. It just

has to be more than nothing. I'll take anything you can give me that even hints at a qualified suspect, but I can't accuse a new organization of terrorism if I have no evidence at all. I promised the archbishop that we would be respectful of legitimate pro-life groups."

"Understood, sir. I'll keep you informed."

The mayor hung up the phone and got out of his chair. He wanted a cigarette badly. Every cell in his body cried out for a nicotine fix. He had quit smoking as a campaign promise, and he knew he couldn't go back on his promise now that he was under stress without giving his opponents fresh ammunition. WE WILL KEEP OUR PROMISES, the message said. "Like hell you will," the mayor said out loud.

He thought about stretching his legs and getting some fresh air, but the almost certain chance that he would encounter a reporter made that idea impractical. He began to pace the length of his office when his secretary's voice stopped him short.

"The U.S. attorney is on line 1, sir."

"Christ almighty. Here we go again."

Father T's niece was right about Defenders of Freedom. The group was founded by two former members of Defenders of Life, an organization that prided itself in its nonviolent activities in defense of life and in opposition to legalized abortion. The new group's two founders were brothers, John and James Caffrey, whose sister Betty had died five years earlier from complications resulting from an abortion performed at one of the clinics now threatened by messages sent to government offices, union headquarters and the media.

The brothers were in their early 30s. Neither was married. Nor did they appear to have any friends (male or female). The two did everything together, and they were avid fans of the city's professional sports teams, especially baseball, football and hockey. They had joined Defenders of Life shortly after their sister died and had been active participants in the organization's pro-life efforts until they broke away about six months ago.

The older brother, John, was tall and athletic with taut muscles and a clenched jaw that made him seem angry even on those rare occasions when he wasn't. John regarded his sister's death as a personal affront to him and his family. He was determined to have revenge—one way or another.

James, the younger brother, was a gentler soul—at least in appearance. He was slightly built and his facial features were almost feminine. James worshiped his older brother. He followed him everywhere and did whatever John told him to do. His anger was not as deep-seated as his older brother's was, but it was potentially more deadly. James had the capacity to inflict pain in a cool, dispassionate way. All it took was a sign from his brother, and James became a wounded viper striking out blindly and without remorse.

But were these two angry anti-abortionists responsible for the computer threats? The information gathered by the city police (with minimal help from the FBI which could only confirm that the two brothers were not in any of the homeland security databases) was inconclusive. Neither brother had any experience with computers beyond playing games and surfing the internet. Defenders of Freedom remained the only suspect they had so far identified, but the commissioner knew they were a long way from making what he liked to call "a solid connection."

The commissioner called Father T and briefed him on what they had learned about Defenders of Freedom. It wasn't much, he admitted, but it was a start …

Father T was in his sitting room on the second floor of the rectory. It wasn't really cold enough, but he had lighted the gas fireplace. The brightly burning flames helped him relax and feel at home. And his quiet time in front of the fireplace gave him time to think.

"Commissioner, who are these guys, these two brothers? Where did they come from? Do we know anything about their people?"

"Our records indicate they're from out of state. Their sister was a student at the university when she became pregnant and had the abortion that killed her."

"And her baby," Father T added.

"It looks like the brothers came here shortly afterward, and they've been here ever since. They've kept a low profile—not even parking tickets—and the only people who know anything about them at all are their former colleagues at Defenders of Life."

"Are you getting cooperation from them?

"You mean the Defenders of Life people, Father?"

"Yes, I would hope they'd be as anxious as we are to prevent these threats from happening."

"I think they are, Father, but they don't have much information to give us. The brothers were something of a mystery even to their former compatriots at Defenders of Life."

"Did they tell you anything about the brothers' decision to break away and start their own group?"

"Not much, Father. About a year ago, there was an argument between the brothers (the older one mostly) and the leaders of the group. The issue was results—or the lack of them. The brothers complained that after four years' effort nothing had changed. The clinics are still operating and abortion-on-demand is still a fact of life. The brothers said they wanted to see real change instead of just talk.

"Did they say what kind of change they wanted?"

"Nothing less than shutting down the clinics and putting a stop to all abortions in the city."

"Well, I share their vision," the priest said in a soft, sad voice, "but as you well know, commissioner, the end doesn't justify the means."

"That assumes we find out what 'means' these two brothers have in mind, Father. As of right now, all we know is that they're unhappy with the status quo. There's no law against that."

"Thank God," said the priest "or there would be a whole lot of us in jail."

Jail was on Father T's mind. He knew he had to act quickly to prevent the senseless destruction of a young priest's life and ministry. No question, the young priest had been foolish and naïve, but that was no justification for ruining his reputation for life. Once accused, whether innocent or guilty, a priest carries that bitter cross forever.

"I dare anyone to accuse me of something I didn't do," Father T once said from the pulpit (to the great astonishment of his parishioners who after 30 years of his pastoral ministry weren't easily astonished). "I'm Sicilian, you know, and there are some things we just can't tolerate. I'll start by breaking their legs and go from there."

"Commissioner, before you go I have a favor to ask. There's a young man in the city jail that I need to talk to. Can you arrange it for me? I need to see him tonight."

DAY TWO.
EVENING.

The city jail was a depressing place. It was clean enough, and in good repair, but the whole atmosphere was cold and forbidding. It never failed to intimidate visitors—as well as those who were there for more extended stays. Father T only went to the jail when he absolutely had to, and that was more often than he liked.

A city pastor is exposed to things that his suburban counterparts never have to face. There are certainly lots of problems in suburban neighborhoods, but they're usually hidden behind closed doors. In the city, if your eyes are open, you see everything—all the grime and refuse of life. The challenge is to keep your perspective and not become hard or indifferent to the suffering of others, especially when it is self-imposed.

Father T was a city priest. Years earlier, one of the then-archbishop's representatives offered him "the best suburban parish in the archdiocese." Father T told him that he couldn't live in that neighborhood. When he was asked why, his answer was simple: "No alleys."

The commissioner of police had made arrangements for Father T to meet with the young prisoner in a conference room normally used for interrogation. The guard who escorted him was told to extend him every possible courtesy, but the priest declined his offer of coffee or bottled water.

The young man was already in the conference room when Father T arrived. He wasn't expecting a priest. (When he saw that his visitor wore a Roman collar, he assumed the prison chaplain had come to preach at him.)

Father T sat down on a metal chair in the conference room and faced the prisoner. "Do you know who I am," he said glaring at him with his dark Sicilian eyes.

"No, who are you?"

"I'm your worst nightmare."

"What does that mean," the young man asked, his voice trembling. Something about those eyes really frightened him.

"It means you have two choices. You can either sign the paper that your attorney will give you tomorrow morning or the guards in this jail will beat you every night that you're here. And I can see to it that you're here for a very long time."

"Why are you doing this?"

"I knew your grandparents. They were decent people. Your grandfather drank too much, but he never abused his wife or children, and he always provided for them. Your parents were married at the Italian parish after I left there, but I knew you, son, before you were born! Your parents' divorce was hard on you children, but that's no reason to throw your life away or destroy the life of a young priest who only wanted to be your friend."

The young man was silent. The priest let his words sink in. Then he said, "I understand you were arrested for soliciting an undercover policeman. What's that all about?"

"I need money, Father."

"Is that why you wanted to see your former associate pastor—so you could get money from him and from the archdiocese?"

"My attorney thought it was a good idea. He said I have a case."

"I've talked to your attorney. He doesn't think it's such a good idea anymore. Tomorrow morning he'll bring you a piece of paper that tells the truth about your acquaintance with your former associate pastor. He'll advise you to sign it, and you'll follow his advice. Do you understand?"

"Yes, Father."

"And the next time you need money, come and see me. I may not have any money to give you, but I can keep you from doing something stupid. Got the picture? Am I making myself perfectly clear?"

"Yes, Father. Thank you."

"You won't be thanking me if you don't sign that paper tomorrow," the priest said. Then he signaled to the guard who he knew was watching through the one-way glass window out in the hall.

The guard opened the door, and Father T headed home. He was eager to see the results of the Italian soccer league match on his satellite TV.

DAY THREE.

Monsignor John Dutzow
*(Father T's close friend, pastor
of a city parish)*

DAY THREE.
MORNING.

The Turiddu family had purchased a home in the country nearly 60 years earlier when Father T was a seminarian. At the time, it was little more than a cabin in the woods, but the family added a sunroom, a garage and a large terraced deck on the back of the house overlooking a ravine. Father T's oldest brother, Dominic, who operated the family's business until just before he died at the age of 92, was an avid gardener. The country house gave him lots of room to grow a wide variety of flowers, plants and vegetables.

The country house had been a perfect getaway for Father T during his later seminary days and throughout most of his priestly ministry. Friends and family gathered at the country house on weekends and holidays, especially during the summer. They swam in the river, hiked in the woods and played games on the lawn. After dark there were card games, charades and ghost stories told in front of the campfire.

Now the country house wasn't used much. Father T was determined to keep it, and he often said that he was going to spend his day off there, as he did in younger days, so that he could relax and read and pray without the constant interruptions of rectory life. But it never seemed to work out that way. His day off came and went, and he was rarely able to get away. At 81, Father T was busier than ever—with his family, his parish and his unofficial, but very demanding, service to the community.

When he arrived at the rectory the previous night, after returning from the city jail, he had a message waiting for him on his answering machine from a long time neighbor who kept an eye on the country house. A break in the water pump had caused a serious leak that the neighbor said required immediate attention. Father T called a plumber—a friend from the Italian neighborhood—who agreed to meet him at the country house the next day around noon.

The Interstate Highway System that had caused Father T and the Italian community so much trouble years ago made the trip to the country house a lot easier, and quicker, than it was when the family first started going there 60 years ago. Strictly speaking, the house was no longer in the country. So much development had taken place all around it that it would be much more accurate to describe the area as "exurbia"—not in the city or the suburbs, but also not in the country.

Father T arrived at the house around 10 a.m. after stopping for coffee and doughnuts at a roadside diner that had been in business since before the family first started coming there. The priest did his usual rounds, checking the alarm system first and then carefully inspecting all the rooms. Field mice had managed to get in the house and had chewed up the rugs in the front room and bedrooms. But the priest found no evidence of human pests—except on the deck where there were lots of cigarette butts and several empty beer cans.

There had been a problem with vandalism a few years back. Nothing was stolen but it was obvious that the house had been used as a place to party. That's when Father T invested in a security alarm system that was so loud it would frighten the devil himself.

Once he was satisfied that everything was in order (except, of course, the leaking water pump), Father T could relax. He sat down on a lawn chair on the deck. It was a cool morning, but the sun was warm, and it felt good to sit quietly in the sun and absorb its heat. Soon, he was napping and dreaming about his home in the old neighborhood, and family dinners around the large kitchen table.

He woke abruptly. His cell phone was calling him back to reality. Father T could leave the city, but the city wouldn't leave him alone.

His caller ID said "unknown" but it displayed the number. He recognized the downtown exchange and guessed that the call had been placed from a government building. It turned out to be a good guess. When he answered, the U.S. attorney was on the other end of the line. (Father T knew that "end of the line" was no longer an accurate expression because cell phones do not connect to land lines, but he liked to use it anyway!)

"What can I do for you, sir?" the priest said as he shook off the effects of his too-brief nap.

"Father, I don't believe we've met officially, but everyone in the law enforcement community says you are a most resourceful man. I was hoping I could ask a favor."

"People exaggerate, but their kind words are appreciated. How can I help you, sir?"

"We need someone to talk to the two brothers who founded this radical organization, Defenders of Freedom. We know they won't talk to the FBI or your local police without an attorney present. Would it be possible for you to arrange a meeting with them and perhaps wear a wire? We think there's a chance you might get them to say something incriminating—or at least get more information out of them than we have now."

"I need to think about this, sir," said the priest. "Have you discussed this idea with the mayor and the police commissioner? What do they think?"

"I have to be honest with you, Father, because you'd find out anyway. They were both very unhappy with my proposal. Understandably, they're concerned for your safety—as I am—but in the end they agreed that this may be our only shot at solving this case and preventing a massacre. Of course, we'll take every precaution and if there's even the slightest hint of danger, we'll move in and take control of the situation immediately."

"I do need to think about this, sir, and I want to speak with some friends. I'll call you back this afternoon with my answer."

"Thank you, Father. As you know, we don't have much time. If at all possible, we'd like to arrange this meeting for early tomorrow."

"I won't delay. I'll call you this afternoon. Goodbye."

Father T immediately called his cousin, Msgr. Cugino, and left a message on his cell phone. "It's me, and it's urgent. Call me as soon as you get this."

He thought about calling his niece Anna, but he decided he would wait until the final decision was made. Then he'd need her help to arrange the meeting. He also thought about calling the archbishop, but before he could do anything, a white service vehicle with Vitale Plumbing painted on both sides pulled into the driveway. Father T got up to show his friend the leak in the water pump. Once he was sure the plumber had everything he needed, he drove back to the city—another trip to the country cut short.

DAY THREE.
AFTERNOON.

Msgr. Cugino returned his cousin's call from the golf course. It was his day off, and he always played golf on his day off—weather permitting.

"What's up? Your message sounded serious."

"The U.S. attorney wants me to meet with the two brothers I told you about—the ones who the police and the FBI think may be responsible for the terrorist threats. They want me to wear a wire and see what I can find out from them."

"Are you crazy? That sounds really dangerous. You're not trained for this kind of thing, and you're 81 years old. What if something happens?"

"They say they'll protect me—that they'll be right there if anything happens. What am I supposed to do? We can't let terrorists murder innocent people. I have to do whatever I can to help."

"I think you're nuts," Msgr. Cugino said. "But I know I can't talk you out of it if your mind is made up. It's a Sicilian thing, I know. But I'm Sicilian, too, and my advice is: Don't do it!

"I'm praying about it," Father T said. "I screamed at

the Sacred Heart all the way from the country house to the rectory."

"Did he scream back? I hope so. You might listen to him even if you won't listen to anyone else."

"I'll let you know what I decide. I still have a few hours left before I have to call the U.S. attorney and give him my answer. I want to talk to the commissioner first—and perhaps the archbishop."

"Will you give up this nonsense if the archbishop tells you to under obedience?"

"Don't ask me that. You know I take my promise of obedience seriously, but there are human lives at stake here. It's not a cut-and-dried situation."

"Well, I'll keep you in my prayers," Msgr. Cugino said. "My golf game has really been off today. I can't see it improving after this conversation."

"Don't forget we're having supper at The Osteria tonight. Our friends from the chancery and John Dutzow will be there."

"I have a conflict at the parish," Msgr. Cugino said, "but I'll see if I can reschedule it or at least join you for dessert. I think you're going to need all the friends you can get tonight."

Next Father T spoke to the commissioner who confirmed what the U.S. attorney had told him. "You're under absolutely no obligation to do this, Father, and no one will blame you if you decide against it."

"I know that, Commissioner, but it's our best option at this point, correct? You agree with what's been proposed by the feds even if you don't like it. Isn't that what you're telling me?"

"I'm afraid so, Father. I agree it's our best option, but I sure don't like it."

"I have one more call to make this afternoon, and then I'll let the U.S. attorney know my decision."

"God bless you, Father. I know you'll do whatever is right."

"As you would yourself, Commissioner. That's the way we were both raised: To do the right thing. End of story."

"Amen, Father."

The next call was the hardest one he had to make that afternoon. Father T dialed the archbishop's cell phone number—hoping that he wouldn't answer or call him back before he had to tell the U.S. attorney his decision. He was troubled by Msgr. Cugino's question about how he would handle being told under obedience that he couldn't do it. In more than 56 years of priestly ministry, he had never disobeyed an archbishop or neglected his duties as a priest in any way.

In fact, the night before he was ordained, his brothers pulled him aside for a talk. They told him that he still had time to change his mind about becoming a priest. They said they would understand and that no one in the family, including their mother, would ever hold it against him. But they also said that if he decided to go through with it the next morning, there could be no turning back. "We'll know how to handle you if you ever disgrace this family or the holy priesthood," his oldest brother said.

Father T never forgot those words. His brothers were all gone now, but that didn't change anything. He had made a solemn promise—to God, to the

Church and to his family. He would never betray that promise. Never.

They say that God has a sense of humor, and that he laughs loudest when we tell him—in all sincerity—what we believe is best for us. God knows that our capacity for self-deception is nearly limitless. That's why we have family and friends (and archbishops) to help us see ourselves as we really are.

God must have chuckled that afternoon because the archbishop picked up the phone immediately, and Father T was trapped. He could not avoid this very awkward conversation with "the boss."

"Archbishop, can I ask you a purely hypothetical question?"

"Of course, Monsignor." The archbishop had had many "hypothetical" conversations like this with individual priests. He found it to be a useful technique for dealing with difficult personal issues without having to engage in conversations that were more appropriate for a priest and his spiritual director.

"If a priest in our archdiocese were asked by the federal authorities and city police to meet with potentially dangerous men and tape their conversation, what would you advise him to do? It's possible that many lives could be saved, but it might also be a dangerous wild goose chase."

"I think I would ask the priest if he thought the potential for good outweighed the risks he would be taking. I'd also remind him that taping a conversation between a priest and members of the faithful could be a breach of ethics. It's not like taping a sacramental confession, which could never be permitted under any circumstances, but it raises serious questions from a moral perspective that would require careful consideration. Finally, if the priest in question were one of our senior clergy, I would ask him if he really thought he was up to such a dangerous assignment. As you well know, Monsignor, several of our older priests are in excellent health, and they provide exemplary service to the Church and to the community, but as archbishop it would be my duty to at least ask whether this task shouldn't be carried out by a younger man."

"Thank you, Archbishop. I take it that, in the end, you would leave it up to the priest to decide. Is that correct?"

"If the priest has committed this question to prayer and has listened carefully to what the Lord is telling him, then yes I would tell him to do God's will as he understands it. But I would also remind him that he should not be motivated by ego or by a false sense of his own importance. There is only one Messiah—one true "savior"—and that is our Lord Jesus Christ. We are called to be Christ for others, but we are only successful with the help of his grace."

"I have prayed to the Sacred Heart, Archbishop, and I want to do his will."

"Then God bless you, and keep you safe, Monsignor. And be sure to let me know how it turns out."

"I certainly will, Archbishop. Thank you."

Father T went next door to the chapel to pray. He wanted to spend some time in front of the Blessed

Sacrament. He didn't raise his voice this time. (There were still children in the school building waiting to be picked up by a parent.) The priest prayed quietly but with real urgency.

"Lord, are you asking me to do this—or am I just being an old fool? Vinnie thinks I'm crazy. What do you think?"

Many years before, Father T had learned that genuine prayer involved more listening than talk- ing. He was not a great listener, but he found that if his prayers were honest, and if was able to be still long enough to let God respond, his prayers would be answered. He believed that the Lord spoke to him— not necessarily in words but in the promptings of his heart.

About 20 minutes later, Father T called the U. S. attorney.

"I've made my decision. I'll meet with the two brothers, but I won't let you record the conversation. I'm going to take my cousin Msgr. Cugino with me. He'll be a witness to everything we discuss. I've learned enough about the law over the years to know that there's no expectation of privacy when two men talk to two other men—even if they are priests."

"We're grateful to you and Msgr. Cugino for your willingness to help us, Father," the U.S. attorney said. "When can we get together to discuss the meeting?"

"Why don't we meet at your office in the federal building tomorrow morning at 9? My cousin has Mass at 6:30. Mine is at 7:15."

"9 o'clock is perfect, Father."

"Will the commissioner be with us? I'll be a lot more comfortable if he's there. He's lived in the Italian neighborhood his whole life. Msgr. Cugino is his pastor."

"I'll ask the commissioner to join us, Father."

"Thank you, sir. I'll see you tomorrow."

"Are you kidding me? You told the U.S. attorney that I'm going with you to meet the terrorists?" Msgr. Cugino was not happy with his older cousin who had stopped by the Italian parish for a drink before their dinner engagement.

"We don't know they're terrorists," Father T said. "That's what we're trying to find out."

"Well you can count me out. Let the FBI and the police do their job. They're trained for this kind of thing. We're not."

"We've discussed this already, Vinnie. The brothers won't talk to the FBI or the police, but they might talk to us—two priests who are known to be solidly pro-life."

"I still don't like the idea," Msgr. Cugino said. He was not a timid man, but he was genuinely concerned about Father T and about the potential threat to his 81 year old cousin's welfare.

"I know you don't like the idea, Vinnie, but I have to do this—with or without you."

"What about the archbishop? Did you talk to him?

What did he say?"

"He said it was up to me, but that I should pray about it first."

"And you're determined to do this?" Msgr. Cugino asked although he already knew the answer.

"I have to, Vince. There are human lives at stake. How can I say no and then look myself in the mirror?"

"So what's our next step—the meeting tomorrow morning?"

"Yes, but tonight I'm going to call Lou Lombardi and Anna to see if either of them has found out more about Defenders of Freedom. I want to make sure we know everything there is to know about these people before we sit down with them face-to-face."

"OK, but can we please go to dinner now?" Msgr. Cugino asked. "Our friends from the chancery will be waiting for us."

Father T was distracted during dinner. His mind was on the next day's meetings—first with law enforcement and afterward with the two brothers. He got up from the table twice to make calls on his cell phone. Neither Lou nor Anna answered, so he left "urgent" messages for both of them.

After dinner, the priest returned to the rectory taking the short cut through the park. He didn't normally drive through the park at night—especially when he was alone—because as pastor he had been called to the scene of too many muggings and carjackings in the park late at night or in the wee hours of the morning. But tonight he was in a hurry to get home.

When he was first named pastor of St. Roch Parish,

in the central west end, 30 years ago, the neighborhood was in turmoil. More than 5,000 homes in this once prosperous community had been sold at far less than their value, or even abandoned, as increasing numbers of black people moved in the area and panicked white people fled to the suburbs.

Father T had faced a similar situation when he was associate pastor at St. Ambrose, the Italian parish. Using all his training as an urban planner, and his extraordinary skills as a community organizer, the priest had succeeded in persuading most of his congregation to stay put. "If you don't move out, you won't lose your homes," he told them from the pulpit and at neighborhood meetings. "The choice is yours."

Father T's efforts helped save the Italian neighborhood. Once again, he earned the name they gave him, *il salvatore della città*. In fact, he was so successful in his home neighborhood that the archbishop at the time asked him to leave his beloved Italian parish to become the pastor of St. Roch, his current parish in the city's central west end. His assignment was to save the parish from the decline that was already well under way.

"The archbishop told me to save St. Roch," Father T used to say. "He didn't ask me to save souls or serve the people. He told me to save the parish!"

Thirty years earlier, when Father T first moved in, the rectory was a shambles and the parish was deeply in debt.

"As long as I live I'll never forget what happened during my first week at my new parish," the priest told Msgr. Cugino and their friends from the chancery as they were finishing their dinner. "One morning very early I discovered a woman waiting for me at the back door. She was bruised and disheveled, and it was obvious she had been crying for a very long time."

"Where were you, Father? I've been ringing the doorbell since 3 o'clock this morning!"

Father T was deeply embarrassed to have to say that neither doorbell—front or back—was working.

"*Povero donna!* Why didn't you pound on the door or call me?" the priest asked.

"I don't know, Father," the woman answered. "I couldn't call you because I'm afraid to go home, and I guess I'm too weak, and too sore, to beat on the door."

It turned out that the woman lived in an apartment just two blocks from the parish. In the middle of the night an intruder broke in. He raped and beat up the woman leaving her for dead. As soon as she was able, the woman fled her apartment and ran to the parish for help.

Father T called the police and requested an ambulance. He helped the woman in every way possible—long after that horrible night. But he never forgot that when the woman first reached out to him he wasn't there for her because no one had repaired the broken doorbells!

"That will never happen again as long as I'm the pastor. Never!"

Thirty years later, the now diverse, multiracial neighborhood was thriving and home values had definitely recovered from the racially motivated panic of the 1970s. But there were still plenty of reasons to beware of strangers in the middle of the night. Just two months earlier, a young woman who worked as the night manager for a neighborhood restaurant was robbed as she walked home and severely beaten.

"Why were you walking alone in the neighborhood at that hour," Father T asked her. "I don't have a car, Father, and I can't afford to take a taxi every night. By the time I get off work, all the buses have stopped running."

"Next time, call me," the priest told her. "I'll ask some-one in the parish to pick you up—or I'll come myself."

When Father T arrived home that night, he scanned the parking lot as always and quickly unlocked the back door of the rectory. After he had turned off the alarm, and then reset it for the evening, the priest went up to his sit-ting room and lit a fire. It was only 9:30, and he still had plenty of time to say his night prayers and read a bit before going to bed.

Around 10 o'clock, Father T's cell phone rang. His was the simplest and most basic mobile phone avail-able—with no fancy features or "apps." He had come to rely on his cell phone, and used it constantly, but he had resisted the temptation to do anything more with it than to make and receive telephone calls.

The caller ID told him that Louis Lombardi was returning his call.

"Yeah, Lou. Thanks for calling me back. Any news?"

I think we caught a break, Father. The word on the street is that a small truckload of plastic explosives was shipped to our city from Joliet last week. I've alerted the commissioner and given him everything I know. He's working on it with the FBI as we speak."

"Good work, Lou," said the priest. "Any way to

connect this to Defenders of Freedom?"

"Not yet, Father, but I'm on it. The truck driver is a Teamster. Our friends at the union are following up with him."

"I appreciate it, Lou. Vince and I are meeting with the U. S. attorney and the commissioner tomorrow. Then we'll meet with the two brothers at Defenders of Freedom. The more we know ahead of time, the better."

"Be careful, Father. From what I hear those guys are loose cannons. I'll call you first thing tomorrow with whatever I have."

"You're a good friend, Lou. Thank you."

DAY FOUR.

Father T enlists his cousin Vince and his friend John to help save the city from domestic terrorists.

DAY FOUR.
MORNING.

Father T was tempted to hurry through his morning Mass, but the new translation of the Roman Missal tied him to the book. He was no longer able to recite the prayers from memory. He had to pay close attention or run the risk of either garbling his words or lapsing into the old translation.

"The Lord be with you," said the priest.

"And with your spirit," answered most of the small group of worshippers gathered in the chapel for daily Mass although one or two could be heard saying the former response, "And also with you."

After Mass, Father T drank a cup of coffee and ate a bowl of Cheerios with a single slice of toast (Italian bread with sesame seeds). He read the newspaper more quickly than usual only slowing down for the obituaries, which he read carefully to see if any friends or former parishioners were listed.

This turned out to be one of those increasingly rare days when he didn't recognize any names among the death notices. Father T was relieved. He had too much on his mind already. No death notices meant no wakes or funerals. And that was a blessing for him and for Msgr. Cugino who were constantly burying current and former parishioners.

Father T was concerned because he hadn't heard from Anna. He called her again as he drove to the Italian parish to pick up his cousin and head downtown to the federal building. Once again there was no answer.

"Anna, it's Uncle Sal. Call me please. It's important."

They parked in a handicapped space in the garage of the federal building. Ordinarily, Msgr. Cugino, who always did the driving, refused to take advantage of Father T's permit.

"You're not handicapped," he would say to his vigorous older cousin.

"Wait until you're 81," Father T would respond. "I'm lucky to be getting around at all. Besides, I only park in a handicapped space if there are several available. I don't want to deprive someone who needs it more than I do."

This morning Msgr. Cugino didn't even bring it up. He was preoccupied with the day's events (and there were plenty of handicapped spaces available).

In the lobby, the two priests ran into two union leaders.

"You're coming to our dinner next week, aren't you, Fathers?"

"You know we never miss it," said Msgr. Cugino. "It's the best party of the year!" It was also the best way to keep their connections with union leaders strong.

"Do you know anything about the threats against the abortion clinics?" Father T asked. "I know you received the threats on your computers."

"We don't, Father. Everyone is very worried, but no

one seems to know anything."

"Keep your eyes and ears open," said Father T. "In this town, there's always someone who knows what's happening. It's important that we find out before lives are lost."

"You can count on us, Fathers. We're as concerned about this as you are."

On the elevator, the priests encountered several parishioners who worked in the building. They greeted them warmly and asked about their families. One woman, who worked as a file clerk for the FBI, replied that her husband—an electrician—was out of work. The two priests promised to pray for him and to mention him to building contractors who were parishioners.

The U.S. attorney and the police commissioner were waiting in one of the conference rooms. The U.S. attorney seemed especially nervous in the presence of the two monsignors. He was a skeptic in the severe style of secular progressives and had no love for priests. He could not understand the deference shown to Father T and Msgr. Cugino by members of the law enforcement community. He was willing to use them to help identify the terrorists, but, as he told the commissioner, he refused to "suck up to them" the way others did.

The commissioner, on the other hand, was completely at ease with the two priests. He had grown up hearing stories about Father T, and every Sunday he attended the early morning Mass at the Italian parish with his wife and family. He had great respect for Msgr. Cugino as a caring pastor and as a preacher of practical homilies that the average person could relate to.

"Monsignor Turiddu," the U.S. attorney addressed

him formally in order to set a serious tone and reinforce his own authority. "We would like you to reconsider your decision not to wear a recording device. If these two brothers are behind the terrorist threats, as we believe they are, we need proof."

"I understand your concerns, sir, but it's not going to happen."

"May I ask why?" the U.S. attorney asked—his voice rising impatiently.

"I've been a Catholic priest for 56 years. I have never betrayed the trust of anyone who spoke to me in confidence. Never. And I'm not going to start now."

"But these men are potential murderers," said the U.S. attorney.

"We're all potential murderers," the priest responded, "but we're also children of God who are deserving of dignity and respect."

"You're being naïve," said the skeptic.

"Perhaps you're right," Father T said, "but my decision is final."

"Monsignor Cugino and I will meet with these two brothers and report back to you everything we learn from them that is not prohibited by the ethics of our pastoral ministry. But we will not record the conversation. Those are our terms, gentlemen. Take it or leave it."

"We know we can count on you both," said the commissioner. (The U.S. attorney was silent.) "Now let's talk about some of the things you should try to discover during your conversation with these guys."

"Yes," said the U.S. attorney attempting to regain control of the meeting. "First and foremost, we need to determine whether these men are behind the computer threats. And if so, we need to know what their plans are."

"The Patriot Act gives us a lot of leeway here," said the commissioner. "We don't need to catch them red-handed, but we do need to prove that they are engaged in a conspiracy to commit a terrorist act."

"How do we get them to tell us their plans," asked Msgr. Cugino, "assuming they have any?"

"Get them to describe the objectives of their organization, Defenders of Freedom," the U.S. attorney said. "Then express some doubt that they can be any more successful than their former colleagues at Defenders of Life."

"We don't know a lot about these guys," the commissioner said. "But the FBI has developed a psychological profile on each of them. The older brother—especially—will be eager to convince you that they can deliver on their organization's promises. That may cause him to reveal more information about their plans than he should."

"Assuming they have any," said Msgr. Cugino a second time.

"You're right Monsignor," the commissioner said. "We're making some big assumptions here, but time is running out and this is the only lead we have.

"The only thing we know for sure is that these threats have been made by someone who has sophisticated computer skills. The FBI's profile on the two brothers says that neither one of them is a computer geek. If they are responsible for these threats, there has to be an accomplice who is a lot more 'tech-savvy' than they are. "

"OK, gentlemen," said Father T. "We know what we have to do. If there's nothing else you can tell us, we'll be on our way."

"We'll have a team assigned to you," the U.S. attorney said, trying unsuccessfully to sound relaxed and confident. "We're giving each of you a preprogrammed cell phone. It's not as good as a wire, but at the first sign of trouble, all you have to do is press any key, then press send. We'll come running."

"Thank you, but I'm sure we'll be fine," said Father T. My cousin and I have dealt with all kinds of unsavory characters over the years. We know how to handle these two brothers. We'll be fine."

"We know you will, Father," said the commissioner—as much for the benefit of the U.S. attorney as the two priests— "but we also know that our professional reputations are on the line here. If anything should happen to either of you, the loss to our community would be incalculable and, if you'll excuse the expression, there'd be hell to pay."

"It's nice of you to say that, Commissioner," Msgr. Cugino said. "We're relieved to know that you've got us covered—whether we need it or not."

Father T's cell phone rang just as the two priests got into the elevator. He looked at the caller ID and saw it was Anna. He decided to let it go to voice mail rather than risk losing the connection as the elevator descended to the lobby level.

Neither priest spoke on the way down, but Msgr. Cugino was visibly disturbed, his complexion redder than usual.

"What's on your mind, Vinnie," his older cousin asked as they entered the lobby.

"This is a big mistake. We're walking into this situation blind."

"We've been through worse," Father T said.

"We don't know that. That's my point. We don't know what we're getting into."

"I know, Vinnie, but what choice do we have? If we wait for more information, it may be too late."

"You're right, Sal, but I still don't like it. I also don't trust that U.S. attorney as far as I can throw him. His motives are political not moral.

Father T checked his voice mail. Anna's message was brief: "Call me!"

He dialed his niece's number while Msgr. Cugino paid the parking attendant.

"What do you have for me, Anna?"

"You and Vince have an appointment at Defenders of Freedom at 2 o'clock this afternoon. I told their office manager you wanted to meet the brothers and learn more about the organization."

"That's an understatement," Father T said. "Thank you, Anna."

"You're welcome, Uncle Sal. By the way, I just found out there's some big money behind this outfit—a lot more money than these two brothers could come up with on their own."

"Who do you think is funding them?"

"I'm not sure, Uncle Sal, but I'm working on it."

"I appreciate your help, Anna. Anything else Vinnie and I should know?"

"Not really. I wish I had more for you, but I don't.

"I talked to Lou Lombardi last night," said the priest, "and he says that some heavy duty explosives were recently shipped here from out of state. The commissioner is checking on it, but so far we can't connect anything to the brothers."

"Be careful, Uncle Sal. It sounds like you're flying blind here."

"That's what Vinnie says. He's right, of course, but we have to have faith. God's grace will sustain us no matter what happens. We're doing his work here."

"You're both in my prayers. Keep your wits about you and don't take unnecessary chances. I don't want to have to make funeral arrangements for the two of you!"

"I don't want you making our funeral arrangements either. What a fiasco that would be!" They both laughed.

" Goodbye, Anna."

"Ciao, Uncle Sal."

Msgr. Cugino dropped Father T at the Italian parish and headed for the hospital to make a sick call. One of his parishioners, a 97-year-old woman who lived across the street from the church and had been an active member for nearly 70 years, was dying. Her daughters called and asked him to anoint their mother.

Father T remembered the lady well from his days as associate pastor. "All my Mass vestments—including the ones I wear today—were sown by her," said the older priest to his cousin. "I buried her parents, and I was there the day her husband died of a heart attack in the parish hall. I pounded on his chest and tried mouth-to-mouth resuscitation, but nothing worked. That was the day I learned how final death really is."

"I'll be back in a half an hour," said Msgr. Cugino, "then we can have some soup and pasta for lunch."

"I'll say my prayers while I wait for you," Father T said.

DAY FOUR.
AFTERNOON.

Father T said his midday prayers asking the Sacred Heart to be with him and Vince as they struggled to do his Father's will. "Lord, help us put an end to all forms of violence and every threat against human life. Help us end abortion in our city and wherever it occurs. But please also help us to prevent the misguided actions of those who want to do good by doing what is evil in your sight."

After he finished his prayers, Father T sat quietly in Msgr. Cugino's sitting room. He felt at home there. St. Ambrose, the Italian parish, was where he cut his teeth as a young priest. If only those walls could talk, what stories they would tell! When he was young, he dreamed of being pastor here, but it wasn't to be. For many years, the "powers that be" at the chancery had persuaded successive archbishops that Father T was already too influential in the Italian neighborhood and that it would be a mistake to make him pastor there. By the time the call finally came, Father T had to decline respectfully, and with deep regret. He was nearly 70 years old, and he knew that no matter how much he loved it, he no longer had the energy required to lead this busy ethnic parish.

Father T persuaded the archbishop at the time to appoint Msgr. Cugino, who was in his late 40s then, as pastor of the Italian parish. It was the right decision— for the good of the parish and its people. But sitting by himself in the pastor's sitting room, Father T couldn't help but think about what might have been.

Msgr. Cugino returned about 45 minutes later. He heated a pot of homemade pasta soup and sliced some fresh bread and cheese from the deli across the street.

"What time is our appointment, Sal?"

"Anna said 2 o'clock. I called the commissioner. He said that he and his team would get there before we do. He also said that we won't see them, but they'll be watching us."

"It's a good thing we trust him," Msgr. Cugino said.

"You're right, Vinnie. He comes from a good family. I buried his parents and his grandparents right here in this church. His mother was a Ruotolo. The commissioner's second cousin is pastor of my father's home parish in Sicily. I see him whenever I visit my cousins there."

"Time to go, Sal. We can take your car, but I'll drive."

Defenders of Freedom occupied a small suite of store front offices in a two-story building on the city's south side. Father T remembered the building well. It was built in the 1930s during the Great Depression as a neighborhood pharmacy. Updated during the 1950s, after the Second World War, it once boasted the best lunch counter and homemade ice cream in south city. The pharmacy had been closed for more than 20 years, and a succession of tenants had followed.

Father T remembered seeing a "check cashing service"

there two or three years earlier. Those places made his Sicilian blood boil. "That's a sure sign the neighborhood is in trouble," the priest always said. "Those places really take advantage of poor people. It's usury—pure and simple. If the knuckleheads in city government, in the state capital or in Washington, D.C., really cared about helping poor people, they would put an end to predatory lending practices. This kind of thing never happened in the old neighborhood when I was growing up. If anyone dared to squeeze poor people for excessive interest on loans or overdue rent payments, two muscle-bound young men from the neighborhood would take them for a ride in the country and break their legs!"

Msgr. Cugino parked right in front of the building. A large sign over the door proclaimed "Defenders of Freedom National Headquarters." The display windows that once advertised "Ice Cream Sodas" and "Doan's Liver Pills" now contained large photos of aborted fetuses and pro-life slogans such as "It's a child not a choice!" and "Abortion kills!" and "Planned Parenthood: Public Enemy #1".

As the two priests entered the old building, they encountered a young woman in her mid-20s who was seated at a large desk with stacks of pamphlets and envelopes. She was stuffing the pamphlets into the envelopes while listening to something on her iPod. When she noticed the two priests standing in front of her, she removed the ear phone from her right ear and said with a sigh, "Can I help you?"

"I'm Msgr. Cugino and this is Msgr. Turiddu. We're here to see the Caffrey brothers. We have an appointment."

The young woman had attractive features but they

were obscured by her body art—the tattoos that covered her arms and neck—and by the dozen or more rings she wore through her ears, nose and lips.

Father T scanned the office while his younger cousin spoke to the young woman. He was looking for computer equipment or indications of the group's hostile intentions. Unfortunately, all he saw were boxes filled with pamphlets and posters. Father T noticed a small laptop on an old type-writer table next to the young woman's desk, but even if he had been able to logon to this computer, the priest could not have determined whether or not someone was capable of using it to send the terrorist threats. Father T was not exactly computer savvy. Msgr. Cugino was even worse.

The young woman did not ask the priests to be seated. Nor did she make any attempt to announce the visitors to the Caffrey brothers. She continued stuffing enve-lopes and listening to whatever was playing on her iPod.

After a few minutes' wait, just as Msgr. Cugino was about to give up and go back out to the car, an inner office door opened and a young man came out into the front office. He didn't smile or acknowledge the two priests. He walked straight to the young woman's desk, motioning for her to remove her ear phones.

"John wants you to take your lunch break now," he said.

"But I wanted to finish what I'm doing first so I can take these envelopes to the post office."

"Do as you're told," the young man said in a sharp, cold voice.

"OK, Jim. I'm leaving now," the young woman said as she quickly gathered her things and headed out the front door.

The young man then turned to the two priests. "Come with me, Fathers. My brother and I have been expecting you."

"This is a mistake," Msgr. Cugino whispered to his cousin as they followed the younger brother into the inner office. Father T didn't respond, but he said a silent prayer to the Sacred Heart.

"What have you gotten me into now, Lord? You better stay with me on this one. There's no way Vinnie and I can do this without you!"

The inner office looked a lot like the outer office—a new coat of paint on old walls with posters and slogans everywhere. A large display window was covered with blinds with thick slats that were very much in need of dusting. Two metal desks were facing each other so that as the two brothers worked they could talk to each other without turning.

John Caffrey, the older brother, was seated at his desk reviewing what looked like financial reports. He stood up as soon as the priests entered, smiled a bit too broadly, and walked around the desks to greet them.

"Welcome to Defenders of Freedom," the older brother said. "We're very pleased to welcome those who share our commitment to life!"

The two priests introduced themselves and shook hands with the older brother. Jim Caffrey, the younger brother, remained in the doorway and did not engage in conversation with the visitors.

"Thank you for taking the time to meet with us," Msgr. Cugino said. "We're pro-life pastors and we're eager to learn more about your organization."

"What would you like to know, Father?"

"We're interested in learning more about your objectives and how you hope to accomplish them," said Msgr. Cugino. "We've been active in the movement for many years now, and we're frustrated by the lack of progress. We hear that you guys mean business."

"Who told you about us?"

"My niece Anna is very well-connected in pro-life circles," Father T said. "She frequently provides financial services to organizations that defend human life. She's the one who made the appointment for us today."

"We're a small outfit—just my brother and me and a part-time secretary—but we're serious about our work."

"What is your work?" Msgr. Cugino asked—a little too abruptly, catching John Caffrey off guard.

"Our work is to end abortion," the older brother said. "We want to put Planned Parenthood and the other abortion providers out of business—permanently."

"Your objective is admirable," Father T said. "How will you accomplish it?"

"We're building advocacy networks in city neighborhoods, and we're teaching people to stand up and defend their freedom."

"Every pro-life group does that," Msgr. Cugino said. "What makes you different?"

"We don't just talk," John Caffrey said. "We act. And we get results."

"Really?" said Father T. "How many abortion clinics have you shut down?"

"NONE! Not a single one!" It was the younger brother speaking, shouting really, for the first time from his place in the shadows near the doorway.

"Please excuse my brother. This is a sore spot for him. I've told him we must be patient, but he insists that we need to be more aggressive."

"I don't understand how a small organization like Defenders of Freedom can ever hope to close clinics that are protected by law and extremely well-funded," Msgr. Cugino said. "What's your strategy?"

"We're not at liberty to discuss our strategies with you," John Caffrey said, "especially on your first visit, but I assure you that we will achieve our objective!"

Every word of the conversation between the two priests and the two brothers was heard, and recorded, by federal agents and city officials who were sitting in a white utility van just down the street. Once Father Turiddu informed the U.S. attorney that he wouldn't wear a wire, a special unit was engaged to plant listening devices and video cameras in the Defenders of Freedom headquarters. Thanks to the Patriot Act, which was passed shortly after the terrorists attacks on September 11, 2011, law enforcement officials now had broad discretion in their surveillance activities when terrorists acts were suspected.

In the early hours of the morning before this meeting, FBI specialists had disarmed the rather primitive security alarm at Defenders of Freedom headquarters and entered the building through the back alley. In less than 20 minutes, the team had installed, and carefully hidden, state-of-the-art surveillance equipment in every first floor room of the building.

The two brothers and their guests had no idea that the U.S. attorney, the police commissioner and two electronics specialists were silent partners in their conversation. John Caffrey's reluctance to discuss the details of Defenders of Freedom's anti-abortion strategy was not the result of his concern about eavesdroppers. It was based on a deeper and more fundamental distrust. He was willing to share his "passion for life" with the two Catholic priests because he knew how prominent and influential they were in the pro-life community and in the city at large. But he was not inclined to disclose any secrets or discuss the intimate details of his operation with outsiders—no matter who they were.

Msgr. Cugino decided to push the envelope. Truth be told, he was eager to end this conversation and get back to his parish.

"I don't think you guys stand a chance," Msgr. Cugino said. "Father T and I have been leaders in the pro-life movement since before you were born. You have no idea what you're up against here."

"You're efforts have been USELESS! A total waste of time!" It was the younger brother, Jim, once again practically shouting from his place near the door.

"Please forgive my brother," John Caffrey said. "He doesn't think your generation has accomplished much. Abortion on demand continues no matter how many prayer vigils you organize or leaflets you distribute at your parishes."

"Go ahead and criticize us," Father T said. "We deserve it. Abortion is an unspeakable evil, and the Lord will hold us all accountable for the atrocities committed in these so-called clinics every day. But nothing I've seen or heard today tells me your results will be any different."

"That's where you're wrong," the older brother said. "We have plans that will end abortion in our community once and for all. Then everyone will take notice."

"You guys are all talk," Msgr. Cugino said. "Without an act of God, there's no way you're going to convince Planned Parenthood and the other abortion providers to shut down. I'm very sorry to have to say it, but I'm afraid these places are here to stay. No one—especially you—is in a position to stop them."

John Caffrey was becoming visibly agitated. The strategy adopted by the two priests was working. They knew he couldn't handle being questioned or having to defend his ability to accomplish his organization's most fundamental objective. He was especially unhappy about Msgr. Cugino's taunts, and although he held himself back with increasing difficulty, everything in him wanted to lash out at the meddling priest and put him in his place.

Father T could see that the older brother was losing control. He decided to press harder in the hopes that he would break and in the process disclose some helpful information. Innocent lives are at stake, he told himself. We must get to the bottom of this!

"You won't tell us your plans, but you want us to believe you can single-handedly shut down the clinics. What a load of crap! We came here thinking that your organization was different. Now we see that you're just like all the other groups: all talk and no action!"

"NO!" screamed the younger brother from the doorway. "Tell them our plan, John. They need to know we're going through with it!"

The older brother was now seething with anger. He

94 | *Father Turiddu*

kept quiet—barely in control of himself—for what seemed like an eternity. The two priests waited. Outside in the surveillance van the police commissioner said to the others, "In this situation, the first person to speak loses."

Finally, at the end of a long period of silence, John Caffrey said, "OK. We'll show you our plans. But not now. Come back tonight at 8 o'clock, and you'll see that we mean business."

"I'm not sure we can do that," Msgr. Cugino said. "We both have parish meetings to attend. Why can't you show us, or tell us, now?"

"You've accused us of being all talk and no action, and you've cast doubt on our ability to deliver on our promises," John Caffrey said. "If you really want to see what we're planning, come back at 8. Otherwise we go our separate ways now."

"I can rearrange my schedule for this evening," said Father T. I'll be here at 8 tonight, and I'm sure Monsignor Cugino will join me if he can."

"Thank you, Father," the older brother said regaining his composure but without the feigned smile. "My brother will show you out."

The two priests didn't talk as they drove back to the Italian parish. Each knew what the other was thinking, and neither one wanted to start an argument.

As they pulled into the church parking lot, Father T's cell phone rang.

"Yes, commissioner. I agree. 7 o'clock will be fine."

"What did he say?" asked Msgr. Cugino.

"The commissioner thinks we should get together and talk about what just happened." He wants to meet us here at 7.

"How does he know what just happened?"

"I'm not sure," said Father T, "but my guess is he was listening somehow."

"Unbelievable."

Father T's cell phone rang again. It was Anna.

"Did you hear the news? Computers at City hall and all the other computers received another message."

"What did it say? Can you read it to me?"

"OK, but it makes me sick to have to read this crap out loud."

"Please, Anna. I'm putting you on speaker so Vince can hear it too."

"OK, Uncle Sal. Here goes:

DEATH TO THE ABORTIONISTS.

WE KNOW WHO YOU ARE AND YOUR LIVES WILL BE TERMINATED LIKE AN "UNWANTED PREGNANCY."

YOUR EVIL DEEDS WILL BE PUNISHED. PERMANENTLY.

WE DELIVER ON OUR PROMISES.

NO ONE WHO IS GUILTY WILL ESCAPE OUR WRATH.

"That's it," Anna said. "Sweet guys aren't they?"

"What time was the message received?" Father T asked.

"At exactly 2:30 this afternoon."

"That's right when Vinnie and I were meeting with the brothers," Father T said.

"It's computerized," Anna said. "It could easily have been created earlier and programmed to be sent at 2:30."

"Creating a convenient alibi for those two creeps," Msgr. Cugino interjected.

"What about the secretary?" Father T asked. "She could have sent the message from another location."

"I hardly think she's bright enough to design a sophisticated computer program," said Msgr. Cugino. "But if someone else did the programming, she could type the message and hit send."

"Even I could do that," Father T said. "Are you still on the line, Anna?"

"Yes, Uncle Sal."

"Vinnie and I are going back to the brothers' headquarters at 8 tonight. They said they'd tell us their plans."

"You're kidding me. If they really are the ones sending these threats, do you think they'll actually let you in on it?"

"We have to find out, Anna. People's lives may depend on us."

"I can't believe the commissioner is letting you do this. He should know better."

"It's the only way, Anna."

"Be safe you two. I have all the monks at the abbey praying for you—and the Carmelite nuns too."

"We're counting on their help, Anna. Thank you."

"Ciao, Uncle Sal. Father Vince, please don't let him do anything foolish."

"I'll take care of him, Anna. Just keep the prayers coming."

DAY FOUR.
EVENING.

Neither priest was hungry, but they ordered pizza and salad from the Osteria and ate in silence in the rectory dining room at the Italian parish. Father T had a glass of Aperol, an Italian apertivo, with dinner, but his cousin declined. He said he wanted to keep his head clear for the evening's encounter with the two brothers.

"Afterward, I'll have something a lot harder than Aperol!"

The police commissioner and the U.S. attorney arrived promptly at 7 and were shown into the front parlor where the two priests were waiting for them. The commissioner spoke first.

"I know you're angry with us for listening to your conversation with the brothers, but it was for your own safety—and the protection of many innocent people."

"You're right, Commissioner. We're not happy about this," Father T said, "but for now let's focus on our plan for tonight."

"Do we have a plan?" asked Msgr. Cugino. "I thought we were playing this by ear."

"Tonight's meeting is a continuation of the conversation you started this afternoon," the U.S. attorney said in his most professional voice. "You both did a fine job of engaging the brothers in a discussion of their plans today. Let's hope you can get them to reveal something significant tonight."

"I'm afraid that all we did this afternoon is make John Caffrey mad," Msgr. Cugino said. "Tonight he'll either be more cautious or more vindictive."

"We know from the younger brother's outburst that they have a plan that they believe will shut down the clinics," the commissioner pointed out, conscious that they didn't have much time left to talk before the 8 o'clock meeting. "All we need you to do now is get them to tell you what the plan involves."

"What if their plan has nothing to do with the threats against the abortion clinics?" Father T asked.

"Well, at least we'll know we have to look somewhere else," the commissioner said.

"With time running out," the U.S. attorney added.

"Monsignor Cugino and I have confidence in the Sacred Heart," said Father T. "He won't let us down."

The U.S. attorney pursed his lips but said nothing. He obviously didn't share the priests' confidence in religious matters, but he was desperate enough to let it be—for now.

Msgr. Cugino stood up—signaling that it was time to go.

"We'll be listening to every word," the commissioner said as he grasped both priests by the arm. "We're not going to let anything happen to our favorite priests!"

"This time, I have to admit I'm relieved to know you'll

be listening," Msgr. Cugino admitted. "We'll worry about the ethics later."

Once they were by themselves in Father T's car, the two priests opened up to each other.

"I don't agree with you about the surveillance, Vinnie. It's just not right. Until we have some evidence that these guys have done something wrong, it's not only unprofessional, it's an invasion of their privacy."

"I hope you're right, Sal. I hope these guys are innocent and we're the ones who are guilty of presumption. In the meantime, I'm not sorry that the commissioner and the FBI have our backs!"

"You're probably right, Vince, but I'm really angry with the commissioner. I expect the other one to be untrustworthy. As we used to say in the old neighborhood, he's not one of us. He's an American. But the commissioner grew up here in this parish. I remember when he was an altar boy. When I say I don't want my conversation recorded, I expect him to pay attention."

"He was worried about us, Sal, or he wouldn't have gone along with it. He's a good man."

"I know he's a good man, Vinnie, but he should have told us they were recording our conversation. End of story."

"Understood. Now can we please drop this? We have a lot more to worry about right now than the commissioner."

As the two priests approached the Defenders of Freedom headquarters, they saw a large man standing on the sidewalk by the front door. He was wearing a dark windbreaker, and he seemed to be waiting for something, or someone. He had his hood up and his arms folded as if to warm himself in the cool night air.

"I think that's John Dutzow," Msgr. Cugino said as he pulled up in front of the building and parked the car.

"Huh?" Father T exclaimed as he strained his eyes to get a better look at the solitary figure standing on the sidewalk.

"John, is that you?" Father T rolled down the window and leaned out of the car.

"Of course, it's me," Msgr. Dutzow replied. "I've been waiting for you guys."

"But how did you know we'd be here?" asked Msgr. Cugino as he and Father T got out of the car.

"You forget that I was chaplain to the city firefighters for 20 years. I know almost as many people at city hall as you guys do. Besides, this is my parish. Sal taught me that a good pastor knows everything that happens in his parish."

"But why are you here, John?" Father T asked. "This is a complicated situation. I'm not sure how the two brothers will react to you."

"I don't care," Msgr. Dutzow said. "You're not going to do this without me. This is my parish, and whatever happens to you here, happens to me as well."

Father T knew it was useless to argue. He would take exactly the same position if the roles were reversed. So would Vince. That's the kind of priests they were trained to be. End of story.

"OK, John, come with us," Father T said. "We'll have to trust the Sacred Heart on this one. Hopefully, the brothers won't mind adding a third priest to the conversation."

"This afternoon we challenged them to explain their

plan to shut down the city's abortion clinics," Msgr. Cugino said hoping to bring their friend up to speed. "They admitted they have a plan, but they refused to tell us anything specific about it. Instead, they told us to come back now. We have no idea what they're up to, or if it has anything to do with the terrorist threats, but I hope we're about to find out."

"By the way, John, the police commissioner and the FBI have bugged Defenders of Freedom headquarters. They'll be listening to our conversation, and they've promised to come running if things go wrong."

"That's good to know," Msgr. Dutzow said. "I like having the cavalry close by."

The front door was locked, so Msgr. Cugino knocked loudly with his fist. After a minute or more, when no one answered, he knocked even louder and yelled, "Anyone home?"

Another minute passed (to the three priests it seemed like forever) until they heard a voice say, "Over here" and they turned and saw Jim Caffrey, the younger brother, standing at the entrance to an alley about half a block away.

"Come this way,' he said.

When they got to the alley, the young man nodded toward Msgr. Dutzow and said, "Who's he?"

"I'm Msgr. John Dutzow. I'm the pastor of this parish, and I've been a strong pro-life advocate for more than 30 years."

"Monsignor Dutzow is a friend of ours. We trust him," Father T said. "He's a good priest."

"John won't like it," the younger brother said. "He

doesn't like surprises."

"We're a team," Msgr. Cugino insisted. "Take one, take all."

"Then follow me. It's getting late and John will wonder what's taking us so long."

The three priests followed as the lanky young man led them down the alley. When they arrived at the back door, there was a black Chevy Suburban parked in the alley.

"Get in," Jim Caffrey said. "We're going for a ride."

"Huh?" said Father T. "You never said anything about riding with you in a truck. I'm not sure I like that idea."

"Suit yourself," the young man said, "but the only way to learn about our plan is to come with me to our warehouse."

"We're not getting into that vehicle with you," said Msgr. Cugino who was getting hot under his Roman collar. "You drive, and we'll follow in our car."

"Not a chance. You come with me now or you stay here. The location of our warehouse is a secret. In fact, if you ride with me, you'll have to agree to be blindfolded. That's the only way you'll get there."

"This is absurd!" Msgr. Dutzow shouted. He was beside himself. "Who do you people think you are—a bunch of gangsters in a B movie?"

"You invited yourself to this party," Jim Caffrey said. "If you don't like the rules, you don't have to play the game. But make up your mind. My brother won't wait much longer."

"We'll go with you," Father T said, "but I warn you—if anything happens to the three of us every policeman in the city will avenge our cause. Believe me, you'll regret it."

"Just do what I ask, Father, and nothing will happen to you. I promise. We don't want to hurt anyone."

The three priests got into the back seat of the Suburban, and the young man blindfolded each one with a thick black cloth. He also bound their wrists to prevent them from loosening their blindfolds. When he was sure they were secure, he got in the driver's seat, engaged the childproof door locks and then drove out of the alley and turned left onto the main highway.

The police commissioner, U.S. attorney and an FBI surveillance team had watched the two priests and Msgr. Dutzow (who the commissioner recognized) follow Jim Caffrey down the alley, but they couldn't hear their conversation or see them once they were behind the building. The FBI's bugs were inside the office building. They were not prepared for what was unfolding in the alley behind the building.

The U.S. attorney was a basket case.

"Why don't they go inside where we can hear them?" he shouted so loudly that the commissioner and FBI agents all reacted immediately with a powerful "Sshh!"

"They'll hear us," the commissioner said with a loud whisper. "Then everything we've done up 'til now will be lost."

"I know. I'm sorry," the U.S. attorney said as quietly as he could. "What do we do now?"

The commissioner shook his head. "If they don't go into the building or come back out of that alley in two minutes, we're going after them. We can't risk losing those three priests. Not on my watch."

But before anything could be done, the black Chevy

Suburban, with Jim Caffrey driving, pulled out of the alley and headed north on the main highway past the FBI's white panel van. The back windows were all tinted so that it was impossible to see who was inside, but the commissioner wasn't about to take any chances.

"Follow him!" he shouted to the FBI agent who had driven them to their current location. Fortunately, the van was pointed in the right direction or it would have been impossible to catch up with the Suburban.

The SUV continued north on the main highway, stopping occasionally at red lights, but making generally good progress because, in the evening, traffic was much lighter than during the day. After about 15 minutes, the SUV crossed over to an Interstate entrance ramp heading west. After another 5 minutes or so, the brothers' black Suburban, which was followed at a safe distance by the FBI's white panel van, passed the airport and took the first exit to the right. A few more miles, and the Suburban turned right into an industrial park that contained rows of warehouses rented out to companies with significant storage requirements.

Jim Caffrey parked the car, got out, checked to make sure his passengers were secure, and then locked the doors behind him. The FBI van drove past the industrial park and turned left into an empty lot that allowed visual contact with the Suburban.

Once the young man was out of the car, Father T nudged his cousin and whispered, "I know where we are."

"What?" Msgr. Cugino replied. "Aren't you wearing a blindfold?"

"Of course I am, but I listened carefully to the sounds

of the city as we passed by, and I paid attention to the direction we followed. We headed north along the highway, then got on the Interstate. Once we passed the airport I was absolutely sure. The first exit past the airport leads to a corporate warehouse district. That has to be where we are right now. My nephew Frank rents a large storage facility here. I used to come out here a lot when the parish ladies and I were going to estate sales. Frank let us store things in his warehouse for free."

"Unbelievable. But what good does it do us?" asked Msgr. Cugino. "We're still blindfolded with our wrists tied."

"Not a problem," said Msgr. Dutzow. "All the years I was a chaplain to the Boy Scouts taught me a thing or two about knots. Just give me another minute, and my hands will be free."

"Not yet, John," Father T said. We need to get into that warehouse and find out what's going on here. If that young man finds out that we've gotten loose, we may miss our only chance."

"You're right, Sal, but all this is making me very nervous. I'll wait a while longer, but I won't stay here all night!"

"I'm with you, John," Msgr. Cugino said. "But Sal's right. Now that we've come this far, let's see if we can find out what the brothers are up to."

The door opened and the three priests heard their young host say, "OK, gentlemen. I'm going to take off your blindfolds, but your wrists will stay bound until we get inside." With that, he quickly removed the cloths and helped them out of the Suburban.

They entered the building by a doorway that was next to a large loading dock. Once inside, they found themselves facing a bank of computers monitored by five young men from diverse ethnic and racial backgrounds— two Asians, an Arab, an Indian wearing a turban and a Hispanic. The men were seated in front of the computer terminals with their backs to the visitors, but as the three priests were led into the warehouse by Jim Caffrey with their hands tied behind their backs, the young men stole glances at them, and at one another, silently communicating their curiosity—and perhaps their concern for the visitors' fate.

"Are you going to untie us now?" Msgr. Cugino asked with undisguised irritation.

"When we get to the next room. My brother is waiting for us there."

"Where are we?" asked Msgr. Dutzow. "Is this some kind of command center? It's a very impressive facility. What do you use those computers for?"

"My brother will respond to your questions, gentlemen. Please be patient."

The priests were shown to a conference room at the other end of the warehouse. John Caffrey was waiting for them. His studied smile had returned, and he apologized profusely for the way the priests were escorted to this facility.

"We can't be too careful, you see. There are many people who oppose us and would love to put us out of business. When we succeed in shutting down the clinics, we'll be hunted down and destroyed."

"We're confused," Father T said. "What are you planning, and who's against you?"

"Let me show you," the older brother said. "You'll be impressed."

With the flick of a switch, the wall on the opposite end of the conference room slid open revealing two dozen video screens. Each screen displayed a different location somewhere in the city. Most of the images were exterior views of buildings, but there were a handful of interior shots of facilities that looked like hospital operating rooms.

Msgr. Dutzow was the first to speak. "That's Planned Parenthood," he said pointing to a screen in the middle of the wall. "I recognize the façade. The building used to belong to Lutheran Social Services in the days when they sponsored a free clinic for people in city neighborhoods."

"Good work, Father," said John Caffrey. Every abortion provider in the city is on that wall—including some very prestigious medical centers. We can focus on just one facility," he said as all the images combined to provide one giant image of the Planned Parenthood building, "or we can monitor each one separately."

"How did you do this?" asked Msgr. Cugino. "It's incredible!"

"Over the past couple of years, we have recruited a team of international experts in electronic surveillance, computer programming and digital technology. The systems we now have in place can do amazing things, gentlemen. We know everything that goes on in those facilities. We can document—in vivid detail—the crimes against humanity that are being committed here in our city every day.

"And what will you do with this information?" Father

T asked. "I don't think our local media will use any of it—especially if it was obtained illegally."

"We're not concerned about that, Father. We're preparing a documentary film that will be shown on satellite TV all over the world. By the time we're finished, everyone will be able to witness—in living color—the atrocities taking place in these so-called clinics!"

"But that's not all!" the younger brother shouted. "We're going to shut down every one of these facilities while the whole world is watching!"

"Huh?" asked Father T. "How will you accomplish that?"

"Electronically," the older brother said. "We now have the capacity to shut off all the power in each of these facilities, to make their equipment inoperable, and to wipe out all their databases. The result will be a complete melt-down of all the systems used by the abortion industry on a daily basis. No facility will be able to operate. No back-up systems will function. Abortion on demand will be a thing of the past!"

"Unbelievable," said Father T and Msgr. Cugino in unison as if on cue.

"But what about the people?" Msgr. Dutzow asked.

"What people?" the older brother replied.

"The people who work in the clinics," Msgr. Dutzow said.

"They'll all be out of work," said the younger brother. "And rightly so. They have no business doing this kind of work anyway. Let them find real jobs."

The three priests looked at each but said nothing. After a few moments of silence, Father T spoke up.

"You said we'd be impressed, and you're right. We've never seen anything like this. Never. I wonder if you'd mind letting the three of us alone for a few minutes to chat. We'd like to compare notes and come up with some questions. Would that be OK?"

"I guess so," John Caffrey replied. "I should check on the team in the other room anyway. Jim, why don't you check outside and make sure we're all clear."

"Thank you," Msgr. Dutzow said. "We need a break. Is it OK to use the restroom?"

"Of course. It's just outside this room to your left and down the hall."

The two brothers left the conference room and, at Father T's direction, the three priests moved closer to each other and huddled toward the end of the large conference table farthest from the video screens that were now blank.

"Speak softly and watch what you say," Father T whispered. "The walls have ears—literally!"

"The brothers seemed genuinely surprised by my question about the people who work in the clinics," Msgr. Dutzow said in a low voice. "What do you think that means?"

"They didn't say anything about blowing up the buildings," added Msgr. Cugino." If they're telling us the whole story, they don't plan to hurt anyone. They just want to shut everything down."

"We need more information, and some hard evidence, before we jump to conclusions," Msgr. Dutzow said.

"If what these guys are telling us is true," Father T said, "and I don't know whether it is or not, then there's at least a chance they didn't send the computer messages. Why would they risk calling attention to themselves and exposing their plan if they have no intention of blowing up the buildings or killing the employees?"

"But did you see those computer terminals?" Msgr. Dutzow asked. If the guys operating those machines really are international experts, they certainly would be capable of sending messages to multiple computer networks."

"So what's the next step?" asked Msgr. Cugino. "Do we confront them with the computer threats or get our butts out of here and let the authorities handle this?

Father T thought a moment. He didn't like being in this situation. Too much could go wrong.

"I think John is right. We need more information from these guys before we're ready to hand them over to the commissioner. Tomorrow is Day Five. If the threats are real, no matter who's making them we have very little time left."

"OK, so what's our plan?" said Father T's cousin with more than a little impatience.

"I think we should act like we're really impressed with what we've heard so far. We should tell the brothers that we want to learn more," Father T said.

"I won't be acting," Msgr. Dutzow said. "I'm really fascinated by what these guys have accomplished. I know it's immoral, and probably illegal, but if they can really do what they say they can—without destroying any property or endangering human lives—I think the potential is incredible."

"The potential for evil," said Msgr. Cugino. "I don't see any good resulting from this. No matter how you look at it, the end doesn't justify the means."

"I know," Msgr. Dutzow said, "but we can be fascinated by evil means from a scientific or technical point of view even when we don't endorse them."

"I'm afraid our meeting is over, gentlemen." John Caffrey and his brother were standing in the open doorway. The three priests ended their conversation abruptly and looked up. They had not heard the door open, so it wasn't clear to them how long the brothers had been standing there or what they might have heard.

"We do have some quick questions," Father T said.

"And I never made it to the men's room," Msgr. Dutzow added. "Is it OK if I go now?"

"Be quick about it," the older brother said as Msgr. Dutzow headed for the door. "We've discovered a suspicious vehicle parked across the street. We think it's law enforcement, and we need to act fast before our plans are discovered."

"What will you do?" Father T asked.

"First we have to get you out of here. Then we'll close up shop here and move to a different warehouse in another part of town. We designed this operation to be portable. Even if all this equipment were seized, we still have back-up systems that can be setup very quickly."

As soon as he entered the restroom, Msgr. Dutzow took his cell phone out of his shirt pocket and called the commissioner. Msgr. Dutzow and the commissioner played golf together nearly every Saturday morning. The commissioner was the one who told his friend about the meeting with the two brothers that evening, and when Msgr. Dutzow insisted on joining Father T and Msgr. Cugino at Defenders of Freedom headquarters, the commissioner gave him a preprogrammed cell phone and told him to call at the first sign of trouble.

The commissioner's instructions were the same as the ones given to Father T and Msgr. Cugino. "Just turn the phone on. Then press any button and hit 'send.' The phone will automatically call my mobile number."

The priest did as he was instructed, but the call didn't go through. The phone's display section said 'no service' and nothing he did made any difference. "Maybe it's because I'm in the restroom," he thought. "I'll see if I can get a connection in another part of the warehouse."

He tried again after he left the restroom. No luck. The entire building was a dead zone.

When Msgr. Dutzow returned to the conference room he found Father T and Msgr. Cugino already blindfolded with their wrists tied behind their backs.

"Your turn, Father. We're leaving," the younger brother said.

As soon as all three priests were blindfolded and bound, the two brothers led them out of the conference room and into the warehouse. But instead of leaving the building the way they came in, they were taken to a freight elevator. Once they were inside, the doors closed and they began to descend. Father T listened carefully. By the time they stopped, he estimated that had passed three floors—making them four floors below the warehouse.

"Where are we?" Father T asked. "And where are you taking us?"

"That's not important, Father," the younger brother replied. "We're getting you out safely and unnoticed.

That's all that matters."

The three priests, who were still blindfolded and bound, were led along an underground passageway for what Father T estimated was more than a mile. There was no way to tell for sure, but he guessed they were headed for the airport. He remembered his nephew Frank saying that cargo could be transported from the airport to the warehouses nearby without having to be loaded on or off trucks.

When they arrived at their destination, the younger brother told them to stand still and face forward. The three priests waited (not very patiently) while the young man spoke into what sounded like an intercom.

"This is Jim. Is all clear above? We're coming up."

"All clear," said a woman's deep voice slightly distorted by static.

An elevator door slid open, and then three priests were told to step forward. As the door closed behind them and the elevator began to ascend, Father T counted three floors. When the elevator door opened (this time in front of them), and the three priests stepped out, they were led to a leather couch and told to sit down.

"Aren't you forgetting something?" Msgr. Cugino asked unable to control his anger. "Take off our blindfolds and untie our wrists—now!"

"Just relax, Father. This will all be over soon," Jim Caffrey said.

"Is the warehouse secure?" the deep-voiced woman asked without any static. She was obviously in the room with them.

"John's working on that, but he told me not to worry.

We've been prepared for something like this from the beginning.

"What will happen to the guys in the van?" the woman asked.

"Nothing. If they get tired of watching and decide to come in, all they'll find is an empty warehouse."

"And what about these three?" the woman said nodding to the three priests.

"As soon as John calls, we'll let them go," said the young man. "They're harmless."

"I'm not so sure," said the woman, "but after tomorrow it won't matter."

"What's tomorrow?" Jim Caffrey asked.

"Day Five," the woman said as she left the room.

*Father Turiddu, il salvatore della cittá
(the savior of the city).*

DAY FIVE.
LATE NIGHT.

It was after midnight before the three priests returned to their respective rectories. Jim Caffrey let them go right after receiving a call from his brother. Father T was correct about their location. They were at the airport in the office that processed freight shipments. The priests were let out behind the main cargo area and told to walk to the passenger terminal and take a taxi. Not a chance, Father T had said. He called the commissioner and in less than 10 minutes they were picked up and taken back to Defenders of Freedom headquarters to get their cars.

"What did you learn?" the commissioner asked after he had determined that the three priests weren't hurt in any way.

"We don't think the brothers are responsible for the computer threats," Father T said. "They want to shut down the abortion clinics, but they don't want to hurt anyone in the process."

"Be sure to check out the team of computer programmers they have working for them," said Msgr. Dutzow. One or more of them could easily be behind the threats."

"Yes, and there's a woman working with them who made it clear she has other plans," Msgr. Cugino said. "She used the expression 'Day Five' and suggested that after tomorrow it's all over."

"Any idea who this woman is?" the commissioner asked.

"We only heard her voice," Msgr. Dutzow answered. "We were still blindfolded when she left the room."

"I think I know who she is," Father T said.

"Really?" his cousin exclaimed. "How?"

"My parishioner is the airport manager. Whenever I have to fly anywhere, she makes sure I don't have to wait in the security line. She personally escorts me through the screening and then walks with me to the gate. (She always offers the use of one of those golf carts, but I refuse. Those things are for old people or the handicapped!)"

"Unbelievable!" Msgr. Cugino said.

"So what does your parishioner have to do with the woman we were with earlier tonight?" asked Msgr. Dutzow. "You're not suggesting she's in cahoots with the Caffrey brothers, are you?"

"Good Lord, no. I only brought her up because I've met several of the people on her staff, and one of them is a tall dark-haired woman in her early 40s who speaks with a deep voice just like that woman. I'd recognize that voice anywhere."

"Do you know her name," asked the commissioner.

"No, but it won't take long to find out."

Father T dialed his cell phone.

"Jessie, it's Father. I'm sorry to call so late, but it's an emergency. Can you tell me the name of the tall woman with the deep voice who works for you? Yes, that's the one. Doesn't she have something to do with air freight operations? Exactly. I need her name and address as soon as you can give them to me. Good. Thank you, Jessie. My best to your husband and family. Good night."

"What did she say?" asked Msgr. Cugino.

"The woman's name is Emily French. She lives at 5920 Highlands Avenue in the west end. Jessie says that she's in charge of all freight operations at the airport."

"Remember the shipment of explosives Lou Lombardi told you about?" the commissioner asked. "She would be in an excellent position to receive and store that kind of contraband."

"What do we do now?" asked Msgr. Dutzow.

"Go home and get some sleep," said the commissioner. "We'll take it from here. You Fathers have already done more than anyone could have expected. Thank you."

"You're welcome, Commissioner," said Msgr. Cugino. "I hope you get these people before anyone gets hurt."

"We'll do our very best, Fathers. Now, please, get some rest."

"You'll call us in the morning, Commissioner?" said Father T. "We each have morning Masses, but if you need us we can all be free by 9 o'clock."

"I'll call you as soon as I have something to tell you."

"Call whether you have something or not, Commissioner," Father T said emphatically. "None of us will rest easy until this whole thing is over."

"Of course, Father. I'll call you tomorrow morning no matter what."

All three priests were taken to Defenders of Freedom

headquarters to retrieve their cars. Afterward, Father T and his cousin rode together to the Italian parish while Msgr. Dutzow drove the few blocks to his rectory. They wished each other good night and promised they would all talk in the morning as soon as Father T heard from the commissioner.

DAY FIVE.
MORNING.

It was a normal morning for each of the three priests, but the still-unsolved terrorist threat and the events of the past evening were heavy on their minds.

Msgr. Dutzow heard confessions for the parish Sisters and then met with members of his finance council to discuss the next year's budget.

Msgr. Cugino had two funerals and a meeting of the Italian American Neighborhood Association (IANA).

Father Turiddu celebrated the morning Mass, had breakfast with a neighboring pastor, visited his sister Jenny, and then met with the principal of the parish school to discuss the upcoming golf tournament to raise money for scholarships.

The daily business of parish life was not interrupted by the terrorists' threat, but the three priests found themselves muttering prayers to the Sacred Heart, the Blessed Mother and their favorite saints throughout the morning. The tension was so thick you would need a machete to cut through it as people throughout the city waited anxiously to learn whether the terrorists threats would actually happen that night at the stroke of midnight.

At 11 am, Father T's cell phone vibrated in his shirt pocket. He was still meeting with his principal, but he fumbled to open the phone and see who was calling. It was the commissioner.

"Father, we've had a busy morning. The Caffrey brothers have been arrested along with the team of computer specialists who worked with them at the warehouse. They're all being interrogated by the FBI now."

"Thank God," said the priest. "Have you been able to prevent the threats from happening?"

"Unfortunately, Father, we're not sure that any of these guys were responsible for the threats. We've questioned them aggressively since early this morning. As you heard them say, their plan was to shut down the clinics using technology. They seem to be genuinely unaware of any plan to blow up the buildings or harm innocent life."

"But there has to be a connection," Father T said. "Have you located the deep-voiced woman, Emily French?"

"Not yet, Father, but every local, state and federal law enforcement agency is looking for her."

"Is there anything I can do to help?"

"Use your connections, Father. We really need to find this woman—today!"

"OK, Commissioner. I'll call Msgr. Cugino and Msgr. Dutzow. We have lots of contacts all over the city. We'll see what we can find out."

"Thanks, Father. We're all very grateful for your help."

"It's what we were ordained for, Commissioner—to save souls and help people in need. End of story."

DAY FIVE.
NOON.

"**M**r. Mayor! There's another message!"

The mayor started to turn on his computer when he heard his secretary scream. He knew it would take too long to "boot-up," so he hurried to the outer office. The secretary pointed to the screen. There was a full-color image of a building being blown to bits followed by the familiar looking message:

ALL YOUR EFFORTS TO PREVENT US HAVE BEEN FUTILE. AT MIDNIGHT TONIGHT ALL THE ABORTION CLINICS WILL BE DESTROYED AND ALL WHO WORKED IN THESE DEATH PALACES WILL KNOW THE FATE OF THE UNBORN BABIES THEY HAVE SYSTEMATICALLY MURDERED UNDER THE PROTECTION OF YOUR UNJUST LAWS AND YOUR CRUELLY SELFISH POLICIES.

DO NOT ATTEMPT TO STOP US. WE <u>WILL</u> DELIVER ON OUR PROMISES.

"Get the commissioner and the U.S. attorney. Now!" said the mayor. "Time is running out."

Within 15 minutes, all were gathered in the mayor's conference room. The commissioner and the U.S. attorney were joined by the FBI's lead field agent and by a specialist from Homeland Security. All agreed that the threat was serious.

"Let's start with the people," the mayor said. "What are we doing to protect them?"

"Every employee and volunteer who has anything to do with the reproductive services agencies in the city and county has been identified. Each has been warned about the danger and advised to evacuate the area," said the FBI agent. "If everyone scatters, there's no way these terrorists can harm them all simultaneously."

"Let's pray that you're right. What about the buildings?" asked the mayor.

"Every building has been checked and rechecked," the Homeland Security official replied. "No explosive devices have been found anywhere, but we're keeping them all under surveillance. No one will get near one of those facilities without our knowing it."

"Why am I not reassured?" the mayor asked rhetorically. "As the terrorists say, so far, all our efforts have been futile."

"That's not exactly true," said the commissioner. "We have prevented the Defenders of Freedom group from carrying out its assault on the clinic's utilities and electronics, and while we're reasonably sure those guys were not involved in these death threats, we do think there is a connection. The airport official who was working with them seems to have known more than her colleagues. When we find her, we believe we'll get to the bottom of all this."

"There's not much time, Commissioner," said the mayor once again wishing he had a cigarette. "Find her. Fast!"

"We're all doing our very best," said the U.S. attorney who had been fidgeting with his pen doodling images of hooded figures just about to be hanged. "We only have until midnight tonight to solve this mystery and stop whoever's responsible. Otherwise we can all kiss our careers goodbye."

"There's a lot more at stake here than our careers," the commissioner said soberly and with more than a hint of anger.

"Enough," said the mayor. Let's find and stop these terrorists.

The three priests had agreed to meet at the Osteria for lunch. No one had much of an appetite, but they wanted to compare notes. Father T had pizza with cheese and tomato sauce only. (He couldn't understand how people could ruin good pizza by adding "all that garbage.") Msgr. Dutzow ate Spaghetti with Meatballs. Msgr. Cugino said he wasn't hungry. He had Italian Wedding Soup and a small salad.

Father T reported his conversation with the commissioner. He explained that the challenge now was to find Emily French and discover her connection to the computer threats. Msgr. Dutzow had seen the latest message on his Smart Phone, and Father T and Msgr. Cugino each received calls from parishioners who worked at city hall, so the three priests were aware that the latest threat had been delivered.

"I called my niece Anna and she's calling Emily French's friends and co-workers using a list I received from Jessie, my parishioner who manages the airport. I also called Lou Lombardi. He's working with the unions and his connections in government to follow-up on the reported shipment of explosives from Joliet."

"What about Jessie?" Msgr. Dutzow asked.

"Jessie doesn't know anything, but she's asked her staff to keep their eyes and ears open. The FBI searched Ms. French's office and computer and came up empty. They've also determined that the people who work for her at the airport are not involved in any way."

"What about her family or friends?" asked Msgr. Cugino. "Somebody has to know where she is and what she's been doing?"

"I just told you Anna is looking into this," Father T said.

"Yes, but does she know where to look or is she just making stabs in the dark?"

"You know Anna," Father T said, "She drives me crazy sometimes, but she's a Turiddu. When she sets her mind on something she doesn't give up until she's succeeded."

The priests' conversation was interrupted by the archbishop and three members of his chancery staff who had just arrived at the Osteria for lunch. The Norcini family and members of their restaurant staff greeted the archbishop and his guests warmly, but they didn't make a fuss. Quiet but attentive service and excellent "home-cooked" cuisine were hallmarks of the Osteria dating back many years.

"*Buongiorno*, Archbishop," said the Osteria's proprietor. "We're honored to have you with us as always."

"How's your father's health?" the archbishop asked.

"Couldn't be better, your Excellency, thank you. We're planning his 90th birthday party. We hope you'll join us!"

"I would be delighted. Call my office, and we'll see if we can't get it on my calendar."

"Of course. Thank you. *Buon appetito!*"

"Monsignors," the archbishop said as he approached their table. "I assume you're discussing the latest terrorist threat. What are we doing to help law enforcement prevent a catastrophic assault on human life?"

"Archbishop, we're doing everything we can to help identify and stop these monsters," Father T said. "Last night, the three of us helped the commissioner foil a cyber attack against the abortion clinics, but so far the people behind the threatened explosions and loss of life are still at-large."

"I'm proud of your efforts to defend life," the archbishop said. "All violence is reprehensible—no matter what form it takes. We have to do everything in our power to proclaim, and protect, the dignity of human life. That starts with the power of prayer, Fathers. Please know that you are in my prayers, and if there's anything else I can do, call me on my cell. I'll respond as quickly as I can."

"Your prayers and support are important to us," Father T said. "We're all in this together."

DAY FIVE.
AFTERNOON.

Father T drove back to his parish through the park. It was a beautiful day, and runners lined the streets and walking paths. The park was created at the time of the World's Fair more than 100 years earlier. It was an urban treasure bordered now by a large, internationally renowned medical center to the east and one of the state's most prestigious private universities to the west. The zoo and the city's museums of art, history and science were within, or adjacent to, this magnificent park, and people came from every region of the world to experience the beauty and vitality of this man-made Garden of Eden.

The park was only a mile from Father T's rectory, but it was light years away from the social and economic challenges many of his parishioners were dealing with every day. From the pulpit, Father T had announced that no members of this parish would lose their homes because of foreclosure. "We are a parish family," the pastor said. "Together, we'll find a way to help each other."

And it worked. Parishioners banded together and saved their neighbors who were in financial trouble because of the bad economy. "We're all in this together," Father T told the archbishop and his parishioners. As long as he was healthy enough (mentally and physically) to serve as pastor, no member of his parish would suffer unnecessarily. End of story.

But could he save the city from the awful tragedy that was scheduled to occur that very night? As he drove through the park, he was worried—and more than a little afraid.

"Sacred Heart of Jesus, you can't let this happen. I won't allow it! It's not right to let innocent people die because of angry and misguided thugs who don't understand that life can never be defended by violence."

Father T's prayer was interrupted by a very modern *deus ex machina*, his cell phone, which rang loudly through the Bluetooth feature of his car's audio system and demanded to be answered immediately—prayer or no prayer.

"Hello," the priest shouted.

"Uncle Sal, this is Anna."

"Yes, Anna. What do you have for me?"

"I found out where Emily French is. She was seen this morning at a loft apartment downtown near the sports complex. I'll give you the address, but you have to promise me you'll give it to the commissioner and not go there yourself."

"What's the address?"

"You didn't promise not to go there."

"Anna, for God's sake, I'm almost 82 years old. Of course, I'll give it to the commissioner."

"8220 Carr Avenue. Apartment 14B."

"Where did you get this, Anna?"

"One of the ladies in my Bible study group has an aunt who lives in the building. She spotted Ms. French this morning and said she was accompanied by two very tough-looking men. Tell the commissioner to be careful."

"I will, Anna. Thank you."

Father T made a U-turn and immediately headed east on the parkway toward downtown. He called Msgr. Cugino, as he turned but he had to leave a message on his cousin's cell phone.

"It's me. Call me. Please, please, please. I know where Emily French is, and I'm on my way to talk to her."

Should he call the commissioner? Father T knew the answer was "yes," but something told him that he should talk to Ms. French first. He didn't lie to Anna. Of course he would tell the commissioner. He just didn't say when.

He was now on the Interstate highway almost downtown. At the familiar downtown exit, he followed the off ramp and turned right at the traffic light.

"You know I grew up here," he said to the Sacred Heart. "It was a ghetto but we didn't know it. It was our home—the old neighborhood—and we were happy. Help me now to keep this woman and her friends from destroying what's left of my city."

Father T parked on the corner of 8th and Carr and walked to the building where Emily French and her companions were seen that morning. It was a very old building that had been completely gutted and rebuilt as loft apartments. The priest's first challenge was how to get into the building. Then, of course, he had to figure out what to say to the deep-voiced woman from the airport.

Father T pressed the call button for an apartment on one of the lower floors. No answer. He then tried another apartment—this time on the 12th floor. (It was the floor below Emily French's because, like many old buildings, there was no 13th floor.)

An elderly woman answered. "Who is it?"

"My name is Father Salvatore Turiddu. I grew up in this neighborhood. May I come up and talk to you?"

"What was the name of the parish church they tore down two blocks from here?" The woman had her own security questions!

"Our Lady Help of Christians."

"Come up, Father. I'll buzz you in."

When he got out of the elevator on the 12th floor, Father T saw the woman standing in the hall in front of her apartment. She greeted him warmly and welcomed him into the living area of her one-bedroom loft.

"I remember your family, Father. I'm Lucy LoPresti. My married name is Barton. I'm older than you are, but I went to school with your sisters at Our Lady's. A lot has changed since those days. I moved back here from South County when my husband died. I wanted to be near my old home which of course isn't here any more."

"Mrs. Barton, I have some urgent business to do here, but I'll come back soon and visit. I'd love to chit chat with you about the old neighborhood. I just don't have time right now."

"That's OK, Father. I understand. Come back when you can. I'll make *fegatini di pollo con funghi* just the way my mother taught me. She grew up in the same village in Sicily as your father."

Father T found the stairway and walked up one flight to the 14th floor. He didn't have a plan. He just wanted to talk to Emily French and find out what she was up to. He had the cell phone the commissioner gave him in his pocket, and his plan (such as it was) was to call at the first sign of trouble.

The priest knocked on the door of Apartment 14B and a man answered. He was a tall, muscular man who looked like he either hadn't had much sleep or was hung-over.

"What do you want?" the man growled.

"I'd like to speak to Ms. French."

"What about?"

"That's a private matter," said Father T.

"Come in."

The apartment was structurally similar to Mrs. Barton's loft on the floor below, but it was sparsely furnished with commercial style couches and end tables whereas the old lady's apartment looked like it really was her home. Another muscleman was seated on the couch watching television.

Emily French was seated at a table that might have come from the airport's employee lounge. She was working on a laptop computer and talking on her cell phone. When she saw the priest come into the apartment, she quickly closed the laptop and ended her call.

"What are you doing here?" she asked with the voice Father T vowed he would never forget as long as he lived.

"I came to find out what you're doing," the priest answered. "You've been making some ominous threats lately, and I'm here to make sure they never happen."

"I have no idea what you're talking about, Father Turiddu, but I think it's very unwise for you to come here by yourself making your own threats. Don't you know this is a dangerous neighborhood?"

"I know more about this neighborhood than you'll ever know, and I'm not the least bit frightened by you or by your big goons."

"You're a foolish old man, Turiddu, and you're going to regret coming here today. Now I have important work to do, and you're an unnecessary distraction."

The "goon" who had let Father T in the apartment grabbed both his arms and led him forcibly into the bedroom. He then tied his arms and legs with rope and pushed him onto the bed so that he was lying on his back with his head on the pillow. He then closed the bedroom door and locked it from the outside.

Father T began immediately to try and free his hands. The goon hadn't searched him, and he knew that if he could get the cell phone out of his shirt pocket he could call the commissioner. Unfortunately the rope was too well tied, and Father T's efforts were no use. Just as he had given up trying, the phone began to vibrate. There was nothing he could do but let it go to voicemail.

The caller was Msgr. Cugino. When Father T didn't answer, his cousin immediately called the commissioner.

"I think Sal has gone to confront Emily French, but he doesn't answer his phone and I don't know where he went."

"Locating him shouldn't be a problem," the commissioner said. "The phone I gave him has a GPS device that will allow us to track him anywhere in the world.

If he still has that phone with him, we'll find him. I just hope it's not too late."

"I sure hope he's OK because when we find him, I'm going to murder him myself," Msgr. Cugino said. "What was he thinking about going to meet that woman all by himself! Commissioner, we've got to find him—now!"

"I'll get on it right away, Monsignor."

"And you'll let me know the minute you've tracked him down. OK?"

"You'll be the first to know, Monsignor."

"Good. I'm going to call John Dutzow and Sal's niece Anna and Lou Lombardi. Maybe one of them knows where he went. I'll call you if I learn anything."

The curse of voice mail! Msgr. Cugino made three calls and left three messages.

"Where is everyone? Isn't anybody answering?" he screamed out loud as he paced the halls of his rectory.

"Monsignor," his secretary was standing in the door-way of the front office holding the telephone in her hand. "Anna Dominica is on line one. She says it's urgent." The pastor grabbed the phone from her.

"Anna, what's happening? Do you know where Sal is?"

"Father Vince, I made a stupid mistake and gave him Emily French's downtown address, 8220 Carr Ave., Apartment 14B. He promised me he'd give it to the commissioner, but I just called my uncle's cell phone and he doesn't answer. I called police headquarters to talk to the commissioner, but they said he was in a meeting with the mayor. I screamed at the desk sergeant, but he refused to interrupt him. Do you have the commissioner's cell phone number?"

He gave her the number.

"Let me know the minute you talk to him, Anna."

"Of course, Father Vince."

Msgr. Cugino was out the backdoor of the rectory and in his car before his secretary could hang up the phone. Ignoring all speed limits and traffic signals, Father T's cousin headed out of the Italian neighborhood and downtown as if his own life depended on it.

Just as he drove onto the Interstate, his cell phone rang. He pushed the button on his steering wheel and heard the commissioner's voice say, "We know where he is, Monsignor, 8220 Carr Avenue, Apartment 14B. We're on our way to get him."

"I'm on my way also," said the priest. "I'll meet you there."

"Park down the street by the bank building," said the commissioner. "We don't want to alert Emily French and spook her into doing something we'll all regret."

"OK, Commissioner, but this is Father T we're talking about. There's no telling what might happen. We need to get to him right away."

"Understood, Monsignor. We're not going to let anything happen to Father Turiddu."

Father T was restless. He had been struggling to free his hands, but he couldn't. Every time his cell phone vibrated, he cursed and then apologized to the Sacred Heart.

"You have to get me out of this," he mumbled softly so that his captors in the next room wouldn't hear him. "I don't care about myself. What happens to me isn't important. But too many lives are at stake here. I have to get free so I can stop these fools from carrying out their misguided plans!"

"Desperate situations require desperate measures," he said quietly to the Sacred Heart. He managed to roll over to the side of the bed and as softly as possible he dropped onto the floor. For several minutes he lay perfectly still praying that no one heard him fall. Once he was reasonably sure that no one had noticed, the priest crawled in a snail-like motion (with his feet bound and his hands tied behind his back) toward the bathroom. His desperate hope was to find a razor or other sharp object that could be used to untie his hands.

The bathroom door was not completely closed. Father T managed to open it by lying on his back and using his feet to push the door. ("*Piano, piano,*" he mumbled to remind himself not to let the door slam.) Once the bathroom door was open, he turned himself around and crawled in headfirst.

Using the bathtub and commode as leverage, he pulled himself up, sat on the edge of the tub and then positioned his feet so that he could hoist himself up and lean against the sink with his back to the mirror. It was an awkward position at best, and he found that there was no way he could get into the medicine cabinet with his hands tied behind his back.

"Sacred Heart, help me," he prayed.

Leaning backward, Father T was able to turn on the hot water and, with difficulty, place his rope-tied hands under the faucet. He wasn't sure what difference this would make (if any) but he hoped that the hot water might loosen the rope enough for him to free his hands. He prayed that the running water wouldn't attract the attention of Emily French or one of her henchmen.

In the loft's living area, Emily French was busy working on her computer while her two companions watched cable television (loudly enough to prevent them from hearing Father T's fall or the running water).

"What are we going to do with the priest?" asked the man who had locked him in the bedroom.

"He's ancient history," the deep-voiced woman responded. "No more interference from him after midnight tonight. I'm thinking of letting him watch the attack on Planned Parenthood from the inside!"

"How will we get him out of here without anyone seeing us?" asked the other man who was sitting on the couch eating Doritos.

"We wait until dark and then put a sheet over him and carry him out like an old rug."

"Can we put him out of his misery first?" asked the Doritos-eating goon?

"I just told you, I want him to experience our hard work firsthand," Emily French said. "It will be the last thing he ever sees."

Father T often said he had a high tolerance for pain. On a ski trip many years ago he fell and broke his arm so badly that it came out of the socket. The priest didn't even feel it. If it hadn't been pointed out to him by another skier, he would have continued skiing!

The hot water pouring over his wrists was beginning to hurt like hell, but Father T was determined to wait until he could feel the rope loosening. The way he had to stand on his toes and arch his back was also really painful, but the priest was determined to "offer it up" for the sake of the greater good.

Just when Father T began to think he couldn't stand it any more, he felt the rope move giving his hands greater flexibility. He stepped away from the sink so he could stand flat and work with the rope. With considerable effort, he was able to maneuver his scalded hands and wrists so that, in the end, he was free of the rope!

Once his hands were free, Father T sat on the toilet and untied the rope that bound his feet. He then reached in his shirt pocket and took out the commissioner's cell phone. "Push any button," the commissioner said. The priest was tempted to press them all, but he settled for "0" in the hopes that if all else failed he would reach an operator.

The commissioner answered. "Are you OK, Father?"

"Yes, but there are some bad characters here, and they're planning to carry out their threats."

"We have the building surrounded, Father, but we didn't want to do anything until we knew you were safe."

"I'm locked in the bedroom, but I was able to untie my hands and feet so I can help any way you need me to."

"Is there a bathroom or closet you can hide in, Father? Get down on the floor in case we have to do some shooting."

"Is that all you need me to do?"

"Yes, Father. Please don't try to be a hero. We need you safe and unharmed."

"OK, Commissioner. I'll lock myself in the bathroom

and lie down on the floor."

"Good. We'll have you out soon, Father. Just be safe."

A crowd was gathering on both ends of 8th Street where the police had blocked the road to all traffic. Msgr. Cugino parked at the bank as the commissioner had instructed. Msgr. Dutzow arrived a few minutes later—alerted by the commissioner just minutes after Father T's niece had interrupted his meeting with the mayor.

There were snipers on the roof and a SWAT team had gathered where they couldn't be seen from the building where Father T was being held hostage. All were waiting for instructions to move-in and diffuse the situation.

Emily French looked out the living room window to the street below. It was too quiet for an ordinary weekday afternoon. She couldn't see anything and that was part of the problem. Normally you'd see cars on the street and people walking. Now there was nothing.

"Something's wrong," she said. "Get the priest, and I'll meet you in the basement. We need to move out. Now!"

The two musclemen got up off the couch and headed toward the bedroom. Their leader grabbed her laptop and headed out the front door to the elevator.

The "goon" who had tied up Father T unlocked the bedroom door and looked inside. He saw immediately that the priest was no longer lying on the bed. "He's gone!" the man shouted to his companion. You check the closet and I'll look in the bathroom.

Both were empty. They looked under the bed and found nothing.

"It's not possible. I left him right there on the bed all

tied up. Even if he got loose, where could he go—out the window and onto the ledge?"

Sure enough. The window was unlocked, and there was just enough room for a wiry young man (of almost 82) to climb out onto the ledge. But where would he go from there?

The muscleman leaned out the window and looked up and down the ledge. No sign of the priest. He knew better than to try to follow him. Even if he could squeeze through the window, the ledge was too narrow and it might not hold him.

"Let's get out of here and go find Emily," he said. He got no argument from his buddy. They left the apartment and took the elevator to the basement.

"Where's the priest?" Emily French asked when she saw the two men get out of the elevator.

"He got away—out the bedroom window and onto the ledge. There was no way we could follow him."

"You fools! That priest has 9 lives. He probably jumped. We need to get out of here—fast."

She led them to a far corner of the basement where there was a panel on the wall. It was just a piece of plywood with air holes that sealed the entrance to a crawl space. The opening was a tight fit for the musclemen, but they managed to get in and crawl 100 yards to another panel that opened onto a basement room in the building next door. When all three had crawled through to the room next door, Emily French replaced the panel and led the men through the very dark basement to a stairway that led to a doorway out to the alley behind the newly renovated lofts building.

Father T did indeed go out the bedroom window, but he was never in any real danger. As soon as he crawled out onto the ledge, two policemen (snipers) on the roof two floors above lowered a harness and rope that the priest quickly put on. They then guided him to the corner of the building where he climbed through an open window into the hallway and quickly took the back stairway down to the ground floor. Before Emily French's musclemen had discovered he was missing, Father T was already with the commissioner, Msgr. Cugino and Msgr. Dutzow at the Command Center that had been established in the bank parking lot.

"What were you thinking?" Msgr. Cugino asked his older cousin. "We've been out of our minds with worry. You could have been killed!"

"It wasn't that bad, Vinnie. Those goons didn't frighten me. In the old days, there were real tough guys in this neighborhood. We knew how to handle them."

"I can't believe you climbed out a window on the 14th floor and onto the ledge!" Msgr. Dutzow said.

"It really was no big deal. I've always been very agile."

Two paramedics were treating Father T's badly-burned hands and wrists. "Anything else we should look at Father?" they asked.

"I'm fine. Thank you," Father T said. Turning to the commissioner, he asked, "Do we know where Emily French and her companions are now? We need to get our hands on her laptop. My guess is that will tell us all we need to know about the threats against the abortion clinics."

Emily French and her two henchmen had nowhere

to go. The minute they emerged from the basement into the alley behind the building, they were trapped. More than 100 city police officers, FBI agents and Homeland Security officials had them surrounded.

Once they were in custody, the laptop was seized and rushed to the federal building to be examined by FBI specialists. The crowd was dispersed and the three priests were told to return to their parishes. The commissioner promised to call as soon as he knew anything definite about the terrorist threats.

DAY FIVE.
EVENING.

Father T cooked supper. He said it relaxed him. The meal was simple: Italian sausage, corn and roasted potatoes. Normally he wouldn't have served two starches, but he had a taste for corn and he had no fresh green vegetables, so he made an exception. A bean salad and, for dessert, Drumstick ice cream cones from the basement freezer completed the menu.

His guests were two friends from the chancery who were eager to hear all about Father T's latest adventure. Msgr. Cugino had a wedding rehearsal, and Msgr. Dutzow had a district meeting of the Knights of Columbus to attend. Both made Father T promise he would call them as soon as he talked to the commissioner.

"Supper will be ready in a half hour. Let's go into my front room, have a drink and chit chat," said the priest.

"What can you tell us, Father?" asked one of his guests. "We've seen the news reports, but they never tell the whole story."

"Well, it appears there were two separate threats. Those two brothers from Defenders of Freedom had a very elaborate plan worked out to shut down the abortion clinics electronically. Their team of computer experts worked out a system that would have disabled the clinics' power sources and wipe out their databases. I don't know anything about computers, but I'm told the plan was truly amazing. Thank God, we found them out ahead of time and prevented their plan from being executed. No lives would have been lost, but the destruction of property and financial losses would have been enormous."

"And what about this other outfit," asked one of the guests. "What's their connection to Defenders of Freedom?"

"That's not clear, Father T said. "All we know for sure at this point is that Emily French was aware of the brothers' plan. She had to have some kind of role in it or we wouldn't have ended up at her office at the airport last night. We also suspect that one or more of the brothers' computer specialists was working with her sending out the threatening messages."

"Do you think she cooked up her own plan—to blow up the buildings—once she found out what the two brothers were up to?"

"I'd say that's a good guess," Father T said, "but I hope we'll hear from the commissioner soon with the full story. And I sure hope he's going to tell us that this contemporary Guy Fawkes plot has been completely foiled!"

As if on cue, Father T's cell phone began to vibrate. He quickly reached into his shirt pocket and answered it without looking to see who was calling.

"Yes, Commissioner. I'm fine. What's up?"

"I'm calling from the federal building," the commissioner said. "Emily French's laptop has been thoroughly analyzed and, as a result, her plans have been revealed. There will be no explosions or loss of life tonight! Also, Lou Lombardi's contacts in the Teamsters' union helped us find where the explosives were being kept. They're now in federal custody—along with the "goons" recruited by Emily French to help her blow up the abortion clinics. The mayor has called a press conference for 8 p.m. and the public will be assured that the threats have been prevented."

The commissioner asked if he could come by the next morning and fill-in the details.

"Of course, Commissioner. Can we meet at the Italian parish at 9? I want Vinnie and John to be there, and they both have 8 o'clock Masses."

"Certainly, Father. I'll see you tomorrow morning at 9 at the Italian parish."

"Come to the rectory, Commissioner. We'll have coffee and donuts."

"OK, Father, *buona notte*."

Father T and his guests had supper in the rectory dining room and then went up to the pastor's sitting room to watch the mayor's press conference. The large, flat-screen TV was turned to the Italian network (RAI-Uno), which allowed the priest to stay current with his Italian and to watch the world-renowned Italian soccer matches.

He offered his guests after-dinner drinks, but they declined. Their attention was focused on the local news, which showed clips of the building at 8th and Carr that they had all seen many times already. Then there was the "perp-walk" scene of Emily French and her two companions being escorted into the federal building by agents of the FBI and Homeland Security. Like the rest of the city (and the nation), Father T and his guests were eager to hear what the mayor had to say.

The mayor stood at a podium fronted with the seal of the city. Behind him were the commissioner of police, the U.S. attorney, the FBI's lead field agent and a representative from Homeland Security. The mayor wore his "serious business face." He was not campaigning now, and he was eager to show that he was on top of this situation. Even his voice displayed the *gravitas* that let everyone know he was "in charge."

"I am very pleased to announce that this afternoon we apprehended the individuals who are responsible for the threats made against our community's reproductive services centers. Thanks to the combined efforts of city, county, state and national agencies, we have diffused a potentially dangerous situation and prevented the loss of any human lives or the destruction of any property. On behalf of everyone involved, I want to express my gratitude and sincere appreciation to the members of the Crisis Response Team who responded to this emergency and made sure that everything turned out OK in the end."

"What about you?!" one of Father T's guests exclaimed. "He's taking credit for what you accomplished!"

"Give him time," Father T said. "He won't miss this opportunity to align himself with voters in the Catholic community."

"I'm especially pleased to note," the mayor continued "that this crisis was averted because of the help of
a group of dedicated citizens who went out of their way
to assist local, state and federal law enforcement agencies in their work. Three Catholic priests, with the assis-
tance of their parishioners, were responsible for helping
us identify and locate the individuals who have now
been arrested and charged in connection with this threat
against the welfare of our community. I especially want
to thank Monsignor Salvatore Turiddu for once again
playing a leading role in saving our city from disaster."

The mayor didn't use the phrase *il salvatore della
città,* but many of his constituents, especially in the
Italian-American community, clearly picked up on his
reference. Father T was once again a hero to his family,
his neighborhood, his Church and his community.

Immediately, both Father T's cell phone and the
phone in the rectory began ringing.

"I'm not going to answer any calls—especially from
reporters," he told his friends. I'm nearly 82 years old. I
just want to be left alone."

End of story.

PASTA TURIDDU
MONSIGNOR SAL POLIZZI

YIELD: 6 TO 8 ENTREE SERVINGS

1 to 1½ pounds fresh cauliflower florets
1 to 1½ pounds fresh broccoli florets
1 tablespoon salt
1 (16-ounce) package penne pasta
1 cup olive oil *(see note)*
¼ cup capers, thoroughly rinsed and drained *(see note)*
6 ounces sliced ripe olives
Freshly ground black pepper
Parmesan cheese

In a large pot, bring 4 to 6 quarts water to rolling boil. Place cauliflower in water and allow to cook until soft enough that fork can be easily inserted. Remove cooked cauliflower from water with a slotted spoon or sieve; set aside and allow to cool. Do not discard water.

In same water, cook broccoli until fork tender. Remove broccoli with a slotted spoon or sieve and allow to cool. Add salt to cooking water and bring back to a boil. Cook pasta in this water according to package directions.

Meanwhile, when vegetables are cool enough to handle, cut into mid-sized pieces. In a large skillet, heat 1 cup olive oil to medium hot, reduce heat and then slowly add some of the cauliflower, broccoli, capers and olives, alternating in partial portions of each ingredient. Stir so that all of the vegetables are well-coated with oil. As vegetables are added, add olive oil if needed to coat all vegetables. Stir frequently, until vegetables are coated and heated through. Add pepper to taste.

When pasta is done, drain well. Pour cooked pasta into large serving bowl. Spoon vegetable mixture on top of pasta, then toss. Garnish with freshly shredded Parmesan cheese and pass more Parmesan at the table.

Note: Start with a cup of olive oil and add more as needed, or to taste. Additional capers may also be added to taste.

Per serving (based on 8): 530 calories; 32g fat; 4.5g saturated fat; no cholesterol; 12g protein; 52g carbohydrate; 4g sugar; 7g fiber; 1,220mg sodium; 80mg calcium.

27525705R00088

Made in the USA
Lexington, KY
12 November 2013